YORK NOTES

THE KITE RUNNER

KHALED HOSSEINI

Notes by Calum Kerr

Longman
is an imprint of

PEARSON

York Press

YORK PRESS
322 Old Brompton Road, London SW5 9JH

PEARSON EDUCATION LIMITED
Edinburgh Gate, Harlow,
Essex CM20 2JE, United Kingdom

Associated companies, branches and representatives throughout the world

First published 2009
This new and fully revised edition 2012

10 9 8 7 6 5 4 3 2

ISBN 978–1–4479–1316–0

Illustration on p. 9 by Neil Gower
Phototypeset by Border Consultants
Printed in Slovakia by Neografia

Ulf Andersen/ Getty Images Entertainment/Getty Images for page 6 / © iStockphoto.com/foolonthehill for page 7 / ssuaphotos/Shutterstock.com for page 8 / Stas Volik/Shutterstock.com for page 12 / Thomas O'Neil/Shutterstock.com for page 16 / © iStockphoto.com/christophe_cerisier for page 18 / © iStockphoto.com/ToddSm66 for page 19 / sheff/Shutterstock.com for page 20 / Fabio Capelli/Shutterstock.com for page 21 / © iStockphoto.com/oscaromp for page 23 / © iStockphoto.com/kilukilu for page 24 / GekaSkr/Shutterstock.com for page 25 / © iStockphoto.com/Aguru for page 26 / Elenamiv/Shutterstock.com for page 27 / © iStockphoto.com/ajiravan for page 28 / © iStockphoto.com/sonnyasehan for page 29 / © iStockphoto.com/dlerick for page 30 / iofoto/Shutterstock.com for page 32 / © iStockphoto.com/tomeng for page 33 / Rafal Olkis/Shutterstock.com for page 34 / Lana Langlois/Shutterstock.com for page 35 / © iStockphoto.com/parema for page 36 / Gelpi/Shutterstock.com for page 38 / © iStockphoto.com/kolapakasunitha for page 40 / discpicture/Shutterstock.com for page 45 / © iStockphoto.com/hudiemm for page 46 / © iStockphoto.com/olaser for page 47 / © iStockphoto.com/ImagineGolf for page 48 / anaka Dharmasena/Shutterstock.com for page 49 / © iStockphoto.com/christophe_cerisier for page 50 / Dzinnik/Shutterstock.com for page 51 / © iStockphoto.com/chrispecoraro for page 52 / Zastol`skiy Victor Leonidovich/Shutterstock.com for page 53 / OlesiaRu&IvanRu/Shutterstock.com for page 54 / Alex Staroseltsev/Shutterstock.com for page 55 / Krzysztof Wiktor/Shutterstock.com for page 56 / Alessio Ponti/Shutterstock.com for page 57 / © iStockphoto.com/Rivendellstudios for page 58 / Goncharuk/Shutterstock.com for page 59 / Janaka Dharmasena/Shutterstock.com for page 64 / pio3/Shutterstock.com for page 66 / © iStockphoto.com/AndreiRybachuk for page 67 / © Indiapicture/Alamy for page 68 / © iStockphoto.com/skodonnell for page 69 / © iStockphoto.com/cveltri for page 70 top / © iStockphoto.com/tunart for page 70 bottom / Gelpi/Shutterstock.com for page 71 / © iStockphoto.com/russaquarius for page 72 middle / © iStockphoto.com/oscaromp for page 72 bottom / robert paul van beets/Shutterstock.com for page 73 / © iStockphoto.com/spectrelabs for page 74 / Janaka Dharmasena/Shutterstock.com for page 80 / samotrebizan/Shutterstock.com for page 81 / Rafal Olkis/Shutterstock.com for page 83 / © iStockphoto.com/KeithBinns for page 84 / © iStockphoto.com/ecliff6 for page 85 / © iStockphoto.com/drxy for page 86 / © iStockphoto.com/MivPiv for page 88 / Pigprox/Shutterstock.com for page 89 / © iStockphoto.com/Goldfaery for page 103 / © iStockphoto.com/skynesher for page 105

Contents

PART FOUR: STRUCTURE, FORM AND LANGUAGE

PART FIVE: CONTEXTS AND CRITICAL DEBATES

PART SIX: GRADE BOOSTER

ESSENTIAL STUDY TOOLS

PART ONE: INTRODUCING *THE KITE RUNNER*

HOW TO STUDY *THE KITE RUNNER*

These Notes can be used in a range of ways to help you read, study and (where relevant) revise for your exam or assessment.

READING THE NOVEL

Read the novel once, fairly quickly, for pleasure. This will give you a good sense of the over-arching shape of the **narrative**, and a good feel for the highs and lows of the action, the pace and tone, and the sequence in which information is withheld or revealed. You could ask yourself:

- How do individual characters and my own responses to them change or develop?
- From whose point of view is the novel told? Does this change or remain the same?
- Are the events presented chronologically, or is the time scheme altered in some way?
- What impression do the locations and settings, such as Kabul, make on my reading and response to the text?
- What sort of language, style and form am I aware of as the novel progresses?
- Does Hosseini paint detail precisely, or is there deliberate vagueness or ambiguity – or both? Does he use **imagery**, or recurring **motifs** and symbols?

On your second reading, make detailed notes around the key areas highlighted above and within the Assessment Objectives, such as form, language, structure (AO2), links to other texts (AO3) and the context/background for the novel (AO4). This may seem quite demanding, but these Notes will suggest particular elements to explore or jot down.

> **GRADE BOOSTER** **A02**
>
> Understanding the use of imagery is key to following the themes in *The Kite Runner*. **Metaphors** and similes often reflect the emotions of characters.

INTERPRETING OR CRITIQUING THE NOVEL

Although it is not helpful to think in terms of the novel being 'good' or 'bad', you should consider the different ways the novel can be read. How have critics responded to it? Do their views match yours – or do you take a different viewpoint? Are there different ways you can interpret specific events, characters or settings? This is a key aspect in AO3, and it can be helpful to keep a log of your responses and the various perspectives which are expressed both by established critics, and also by classmates, your teacher or other readers.

REFERENCES AND SOURCES

You will be expected to draw on critics' comments, or refer to source information from the period in which the novel is set or the present. Make sure you make accurate, clear notes of writers or sources you have used, for example noting down titles of works, authors' names, website addresses, dates, etc. You may not have to reference all these things when you respond to a text, but knowing the source of your information will allow you to go back to it, if need be – and to check its accuracy and relevance.

REVISING FOR AND RESPONDING TO AN ASSESSED TASK OR EXAM QUESTION

The structure and the contents of these Notes are designed to help to give you the relevant information or ideas you need to answer tasks you have been set. First, work out the key words or ideas from the task (for example, 'form', 'Chapter 3', 'Hassan', etc), then read the relevant parts of the Notes that relate to these terms or words, selecting what is useful for revision or written response. Then, turn to **Part Six: Grade Booster** for help in formulating your actual response.

THE KITE RUNNER IN CONTEXT

KHALED HOSSEINI

- Born in Kabul, Afghanistan, on 4 March 1965.
- Moved to Paris with family in 1976 because of his father's work. His father was a diplomat and his mother was a high-school teacher.
- Family granted asylum in USA in September 1980 because of the communist overthrow of the Afghan government. They settled in San Jose, California.
- Graduated from Independence High School in San Jose in 1984 and went on to study biology at Santa Clara University, near San Jose.
- Graduated from Santa Clara in 1988 and enrolled in the School of Medicine at the San Diego campus of the University of California.
- Granted his medical licence in 1993; resident at Cedars-Sinai Hospital in Los Angeles until 1996; practised as a doctor until 2004, specialising in internal medicine.
- In 2001, while still a practising doctor, started writing the novel which would become *The Kite Runner*: published in 2003 by Bloomsbury Publishing Plc.
- Became a Goodwill Envoy for the United Nations High Commission for Refugees (UNHCR) in 2006, using his success to aid various projects contributing to the rebuilding of Afghanistan.
- A second novel, *A Thousand Splendid Suns*, published by Riverhead Books in May 2007.
- Currently lives in northern California with his wife and their two children.

CONTEXT **A04**

The United Nations High Commission for Refugees (UNHCR) dedicates itself to the protection of refugees around the world, helping them to return safely to their homelands, or to resettle in other countries.

AFGHANISTAN AND POST-COLONIAL WRITING

Although much of *The Kite Runner* is set in the recent past, covering the last thirty to forty years, it also refers to events dating back as far as the Third Anglo-Afghan war of 1919, and the assumption of the throne by Zahir Shah in 1933.

The country had a period of relative peace until the 1973 coup which features early on in *The Kite Runner*. Following that event, society broke down in Afghanistan, prompting the Russians to invade in 1979. They remained in charge of the country until the collapse of the USSR at the beginning of the 1990s meant that the cost of the occupation could no longer be sustained.

CONTEXT **A04**

Hosseini often refers to Russians in the novel although at the time they would have been forces of the Soviet Union.

In the chaos following the withdrawal of the Russian troops, Afghanistan dissolved into civil war with one particular group – the Taliban – slowly assuming control of much of the country. They were finally overthrown in the conflict that followed the attacks in the USA on 11 September 2001.

(More details of the complex history of Afghanistan in the twentieth and early twenty-first centuries can be found in **Part Five: Historical background**.)

CONTEXT **A04**

On 11 September 2001, terrorists hijacked American planes and flew them into the two towers of the Word Trade Center in New York and the Pentagon in Washington. This led to the USA and its allies invading Afghanistan later in 2001 in an attempt to find those responsible.

However, as well as involving much of this history, *The Kite Runner* can also be seen as a **contemporary novel**. Since the events of 11 September 2001, international attention has been focused on Afghanistan and its political situation. This novel gives an insight into the path that has led to Afghanistan's current position and attempts to explore some of the less-well-known aspects of the country's cultural life.

Although large sections of *The Kite Runner* are set in the USA, the novel is intimately tied up with the culture of Afghanistan and its ethnic and religious groups, both as these exist in Afghanistan itself, and also as they exist in the wider world where Afghan refugees have congregated. The study of fiction regarding immigrant groups living in other countries is one aspect of **post-colonial** literary theory.

(More details of how post-colonial criticism relates to *The Kite Runner* can be found in **Part Five: Critical debates**.)

KEY ISSUES

The protagonist of the novel, Amir, tells his story as a way of redeeming the mistakes he made as a child, and to rid himself of the guilt he has felt ever since. He can be seen as an **unreliable narrator** because his view is skewed or biased by his personal feelings about the events he is relating. The novel should therefore be read with this in mind and the reader should attempt to decipher the reality of events from Amir's sometimes partial telling of the story. The use of the unreliable narrator is common in **postmodernism**. This is a literary movement, which is also covered in **Part Five: Critical debates**.

As well as being an engrossing tale of a man growing up in the turmoil of Afghanistan and, later, as an immigrant in the USA, *The Kite Runner* is at times a challenging and disturbing novel. The main event of the novel is a dark and upsetting one, and later sections of the novel contain graphic descriptions of the treatment of Afghani citizens by the Taliban.

Racial discrimination against the Hazara people by the dominant Pashtuns is also a theme. However, Khaled Hosseini does not use these elements simply to shock or to entertain. They are crucial elements in the formation of the characters of Amir; his father, Baba and his friend Hassan; and in the journey that Amir takes across the course of the novel.

The Kite Runner has had a remarkable success for what, on the surface, seems to be quite a simple and straightforward story. However, the time at which it was written – in the immediate aftermath of the 11 September attacks – and the subsequent wars in Afghanistan and Iraq, have made it a novel which has caught the public imagination. It contains much information which was new to readers in the West and provides an alternative, and more personal, perspective to that provided by politicians and news organisations. In addition, it is a novel that encourages further research into the historical events described within it as well as being an engrossing personal tale of family and friends. As a result, it is a rich text that rewards repeated readings and provides many different interpretations.

CONTEXT A03

The literary movement known as post-colonialism has grown up largely following the dismantling of the British Empire and the withdrawal of other colonial governments from a wide variety of countries. Inhabitants of these countries have used their new independence either to write about the experience of being colonised, or to move to the former colonising country and write about the experience from a distance.

CHECK THE BOOK A03

Stevens the butler in Kazuo Ishiguro's novel *The Remains of the Day* (Faber & Faber, 1989) is an example of an unreliable narrator. In one scene we only find out that Stevens is crying because of the comments of other characters (p. 105).

CONTEXT A04

A kite runner is someone who runs after the free-flying kites released during a kite fight. The rescued kite is kept by the winner of the fight as a trophy. Kite fighting is a popular sport in a number of Asian countries.

SETTING

The **narrator** of *The Kite Runner* is Amir, an Afghan citizen who, as a boy, escapes the fighting in Afghanistan to travel with his father to the USA. He has grown into an adult in America and tells his story from this point of view. However, his story tells of events in his life from his early childhood through to his present time. The character is an author and he tells us his story in an attempt to understand and reconcile the events in his life and his relationships. Both the historical setting and the locations of Afghanistan and the USA could be seen as simple 'window dressing' to a quite traditional story. However, the time and place are crucial to forming both Amir himself and his relationships with the people around him. As such, the settings are inseparable from the story.

Key settings:

● Kabul, Afghanistan

● Bamiyan and Jalalabad, Afghanistan

● Islamabad and Peshawar, Pakistan

● San Francisco, USA

● San Jose and Fremont, USA

The locations of these key settings can be found on the map on the facing page.

CHECK THE FILM **A03**

Although the opening of the film is somewhat different to that of the novel, the film is a remarkably faithful adaptation.

NOTE ON THE TEXT AND THE FILM

The Kite Runner was first published in 2003 by Riverhead Books, a division of Penguin Books (USA). It has been published in the UK by Bloomsbury Press Plc, London, in hardback and paperback; and in 2007 in a special edition to tie in with the film version. Audio, illustrated and e-book versions are also available.

A film of *The Kite Runner* was released in 2007 to a mixed reception. It was nominated for thirteen different awards of varying prominence and won three of them. The film was banned in Afghanistan because of the rape scene and the depiction of ethnic tensions.

LOCATIONS IN *THE KITE RUNNER*

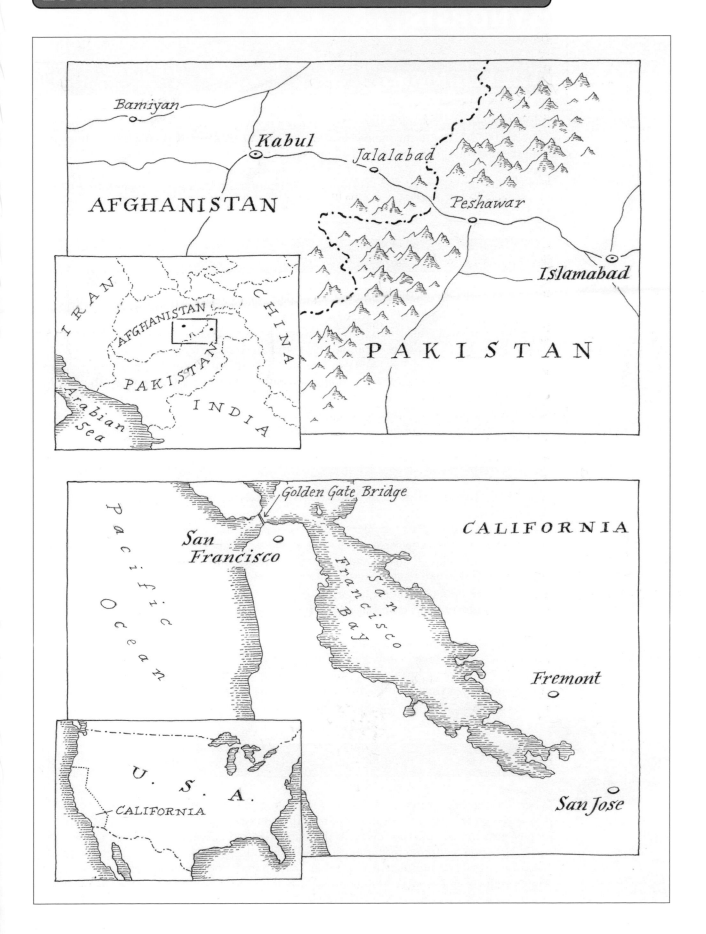

SYNOPSIS

THE BEGINNING

The Kite Runner is divided into twenty-five chapters and spans nearly thirty years. It begins in December 2001 with the main character and **narrator**, Amir, remembering a phone call from the previous June. Amir is an Afghan emigrant who now lives in San Francisco. The phone call was from an old friend of his father, a man called Rahim Khan, who asked Amir to come to Pakistan to see him. This triggered memories of Amir's childhood. Amir goes on to relate the story of his life.

INTO THE PAST

Amir and his father, Baba, live in a large house in a prosperous part of Kabul. They have two servants, Ali and his son, Hassan. Amir's mother is dead, having died giving birth to Amir. Ali's wife is also absent, having run away just five days after Hassan's birth. Ali and Hassan are part of a minority ethnic group in Afghanistan, the Hazara, and are looked down on because of this. Baba and Amir belong to the Pashtun, the majority group. Amir and Hassan are constant childhood companions, playing together and getting into trouble together. Whenever trouble arises however, whether it is a scolding from Ali or being threatened by bullies, it is Hassan who always protects Amir rather than the other way around: on one occasion Hassan threatens a bully called Assef with his slingshot.

CHILDHOOD

Baba is a greatly respected member of Kabul society, partly for his talent for business, but largely for his charismatic personality. Amir, however, is something of a disappointment to him, lacking his self-confidence and love of sport. Amir's interests lie instead with the written word. He often reads stories to Hassan and, one day, makes up his own. Hassan likes this story so much that Amir starts to write down his stories. His father is not impressed, but Amir gets encouragement from Rahim Khan. The one thing that does bring Amir and his father together is kite fighting. Amir is an accomplished kite fighter and Hassan is very talented at predicting where the defeated kites will land, making him the 'kite runner' of the novel's title. Each winter in Kabul there are kite-fighting tournaments and in 1975 it is being held in Amir's neighbourhood. Amir sees this as a good chance to impress his father. He wins the tournament and Hassan runs for the final defeated kite, but fails to return.

THE ALLEY

When Amir goes in search of Hassan he finds him trapped in an alley by a group of bullies, one of whom is Assef, who proceeds to rape the young servant. Amir is too frightened to do anything to help and runs away. Amir and Hassan never speak of the event in the alley, but Amir's guilt leads to him shunning Hassan's friendship and finally to him framing Hassan for theft. As a result, Ali and Hassan leave Baba's house, much to Baba's distress. Amir's guilt continues to affect him for the rest of his life.

CRITICAL VIEWPOINT A03

Think about Amir and Hassan's relationship. Initially it is portrayed as being similar to brotherhood, which is cemented later in the text when they are actually shown to be half-brothers.

CHECK THE BOOK A03

Another novel in which a key event in the narrator's childhood affects the rest of their life is *Great Expectations* by Charles Dickens (1860–1).

AMERICA

The story moves to 1981 and Baba and Amir are forced to escape from an Afghanistan which has been invaded by the Russian army. They make their way to Pakistan and then on to the USA where they settle in Fremont, California. Once there Baba takes whatever jobs he can get while Amir goes to high school and then on to college to study creative writing. They spend their weekends buying items from garage sales and then selling them on from a stall in the Afghan section of the San Jose flea market, a place where Baba can mingle with his own people. It is at this market that Amir meets his future wife, Soraya. Baba falls ill with what turns out to be lung cancer. Amir and Soraya marry swiftly and she helps Amir nurse his father during his final weeks. The young couple then move into their own house and try to start a family but find that they are unable to have children. Meanwhile, Amir secures a publishing deal for his first novel.

RETURN TO AFGHANISTAN

In June 2001, Rahim Khan calls Amir. He informs Amir that he can finally make up for the events of the past, so Amir goes to Pakistan to see him. Rahim Khan has left Kabul to come to Pakistan because he is seriously ill. He wants to see Amir one last time and to ask a favour of him, but first he relates the story of his life since they last saw each other. Rahim Khan remained in Baba's house during the Russian invasion and the subsequent rule of the Taliban. When he learned of Baba's death, a feeling of loneliness led him to seek out Hassan. Rahim Khan found him and brought him and his wife back to Kabul to live with him. Shortly afterwards, Hassan's mother returned and lived with them for the four years until her death, becoming part of the family once again. Hassan's wife gave birth to a boy named Sohrab. When his illness struck, Rahim Khan decided to go to Pakistan for medical help. Shortly afterwards Hassan and his wife were executed by the Taliban.

> **CONTEXT** **A04**
>
> Kite flying was banned in Afghanistan by the Taliban, an extremist Islamic group who ran most of the country from around 1994 until late 2001. They were known for their violence, extreme punishments and poor treatment of women.

A QUEST FOR REDEMPTION

Rahim Khan does, however, have a letter for Amir from Hassan and a favour to ask of him. Sohrab has been placed in an orphanage in Kabul and Rahim Khan wants Amir to retrieve him and place him with a foster family in Peshawar. At first Amir refuses but then Rahim Khan reveals that Hassan was actually Baba's son, making Hassan Amir's half-brother and Sohrab Amir's nephew. Amir finally agrees, seeing a chance to lay his demons to rest, and travels in disguise back to Kabul. The country, and the city, have been devastated by nearly thirty years of war. Amir finds the orphanage but Sohrab has been sold to a high-ranking member of the Taliban.

THE BATTLE

The next day Amir finds the high-ranking Taliban member stoning people to death during the half-time break at a football match. Amir arranges to meet the man, who does indeed have Sohrab, but who then reveals himself to be Assef, the bully who raped Hassan all those years ago. Assef tells Amir that he can take Sohrab but he needs to fight for him. Amir agrees and suffers a terrible beating. He is saved, however, by Sohrab shooting Assef in the eye with his slingshot.

RETURN HOME

As Amir recovers in Peshawar, he discovers that there is no adoptive family for Sohrab and so he offers to take the boy back to the USA. However, when this proves problematic he admits that Sohrab might need to go back into an orphanage for a time. This so upsets Sohrab that he attempts suicide. Amir manages to take the boy back to the USA with him, but the trauma that Sohrab has suffered leaves him mute and unresponsive. He is finally brought out of himself at the end of the novel when he and Amir successfully engage in a bout of kite fighting in a Fremont park.

CHAPTER 1

SUMMARY

- Amir, the narrator and main character of the novel, tells us about a phone call he received six months earlier. It was from his father's old friend Rahim Khan, asking him to come to Pakistan.
- After the call, he took a walk in Golden Gate Park in San Francisco, where he now lives, and watched kites being flown.
- He remembered his boyhood friend Hassan, a kite runner with a cleft lip, and he remembered an event from his childhood in Afghanistan in which he watched something take place in an alley.
- He thought about how that event moulded him as a person.

ANALYSIS

LOOKING BACK

The short opening chapter allows us to understand the timeline of the story to come. It shows us that the story is being told from its end point after the events have taken place. The story is being told in December 2001, but we are immediately referred back, first to a phone call in the previous summer, and then to events that occurred in 1975. The rest of the story is therefore told as a series of extended **flashbacks**. The **narrator** is talking to us after the end of the story at a point where he already knows how it ends, and this fact colours the rest of the **narrative**. Such a technique allows the narrator to **foreshadow** events which have not yet occurred, building **dramatic tension**.

THE IMPORTANCE OF NAMES

Alongside Amir, four other characters are mentioned in this chapter – Rahim Khan; Hassan; Hassan's father, Ali; and Amir's father, Baba. The inclusion of these names in this short first chapter lets the reader know that they will be key characters in the story.

THE KITE RUNNER

Kites are also mentioned in this chapter, immediately reminding us of the novel's title. Amir's sighting of them in San Francisco is what takes him back to his memories of Kabul and, more specifically, his thoughts of Hassan, whom he names 'the harelipped kite runner' (p. 1). This identifies Hassan as the kite runner of the title and lets the reader know that of the characters mentioned, Hassan will be the most significant for the progression of the story (see **Characters: Hassan**).

STUDY FOCUS: THE NARRATOR · A02

This novel is mostly told to us by its central character, who we find out at the end of Chapter 2 is named Amir. This is a **first-person narrative** which shows only Amir's version of events rather than those of the other characters. This means that the events we are shown in the novel are all coloured by Amir's personal reactions and emotions rather than being from an objective viewpoint. The possibility that he might not be telling us the objective truth makes him an **unreliable narrator**.

PAINTING WITH WORDS

The language that Amir uses when he recalls the past carries a great deal of emotion. He talks about how you can 'bury' the past and how it 'claws its way out' (p. 1). This invokes an **image** of something dead rising from its grave. He also recalls words from his phone call with Rahim Khan, *There is a way to be good again* (p. 2). This line suggests that the events of the past include something for which Amir needs to atone. The indications are that the narrative will follow Amir's search for redemption for his earlier actions. We are not yet told what these actions might be, but the repeated mention of 'peeking into the alley' (p. 1) in Kabul in 1975 acts to **foreshadow** events and informs the reader that this will be a key incident in the story (see **Themes: Redemption**).

WATCHING THE WEATHER

Another language technique employed here is **pathetic fallacy**. This is where the author uses the weather to reflect the character's feelings. In this case, the day in 1975 when his life changed is described by Amir as 'a frigid overcast day' (p. 1), reflecting the oppressive and chilling emotions he experienced at that time.

GLOSSARY

1   **frigid** cold, icy, also lacking in affection or warmth of feeling

harelipped a birth defect where the lip and/or the palate of the baby have not fused. This leads to a gap in the upper lip. The term 'harelipped' is no longer used, with 'cleft lip' or 'cleft palate' being preferred

3   **Kabul** capital city of Afghanistan

REVISION FOCUS: TASK 1 · A02

How far do you agree with the following statements?

● Amir is the most important character in the novel.

● *The Kite Runner* is told from Amir's point of view, based on his memories and emotions, and we cannot entirely trust what he tells us.

Try writing opening paragraphs for essays based on these discussion points. Set out your arguments clearly.

CONTEXT · A04

Kite fighting had always been a traditional sport in Afghanistan until it was banned by the Taliban in 1996. Following the overthrow of the Taliban in 2001, Afghans enthusiastically returned to kite fighting.

CRITICAL VIEWPOINT · A03

The presence of an unreliable narrator categorises *The Kite Runner* as a postmodern text. Postmodern works often attempt to unsettle the reader or examine the meaning of texts.

CHAPTER 2

SUMMARY

- Amir looks back and recalls that his friend Hassan, a family servant, was from a lower ethnic group, the Hazara.
- Amir remembers how he and Hassan would get into trouble with Amir's father, Baba, and Hassan would take the blame.
- We learn that Amir's mother died giving birth to him, and that Hassan's mother left her husband five days after giving birth to Hassan.
- We learn that Hassan's father Ali suffered from polio.
- Amir discovers that for a long time the Hazaras have been persecuted by his own people, the Pashtuns.

ANALYSIS

IMAGES OF THE PAST

Chapter 2 takes us back to events of Amir's childhood and introduces us properly to the character of Hassan. Following the indications of his significance in Chapter 1, the way in which Hassan is described in Chapter 2 shows us that he is important both to the Amir of the past, and also to the man Amir has become.

Amir describes his old friend using poetic **imagery** – 'a face like a Chinese doll chiseled from hardwood … eyes that looked, depending on the light, gold, green, even sapphire' (p. 3) – which expresses the love that he still feels for Hassan. This use of **lyrical** language occurs throughout the novel, often associated with significant characters such as Hassan, but also with key places such as the Kabul of Amir's childhood memories.

CHILDHOOD FRIENDS

Amir tells of the times when he and Hassan would get into trouble and how, when they were caught, Hassan would take the blame for their antics. This relates to events that come later, including Amir's reaction to the crucial event in the alley. It shows how their relationship is based on Hassan's unquestioning loyalty to his friend, and Amir's somewhat more uncertain feelings about a friend who is also a servant. This is further reinforced when Amir reveals the first words spoken by the boys as babies: Amir's was his father's name, while Hassan's was 'Amir'.

A DISAPPROVING FATHER

This chapter also introduces us, for the first time, to Baba, Amir's father, who is a powerful man. Amir explains how he wished to spend time with his father, but that Baba would ask Amir to leave and 'read one of those books of yours' (p. 4). Just as Amir's descriptions of his experiences with Hassan set a pattern for their relationship, so his first descriptions of his father do the same thing. We are shown early signs of Amir's attempts to gain his father's approval, and the way in which Baba views Amir's intellectual abilities as being a sign of weakness (see **Themes: Fathers and sons**).

CONTEXT **A04**

Polio, officially poliomyelitis, is an acute viral infectious disease. It affects the central nervous system and causes muscle weakness and paralysis. Since the first vaccine for the virus was developed in 1952 there has been a radical drop in the number of cases of polio worldwide. One of the countries where the infection is still active is Afghanistan.

CONTEXT **A04**

Amir refers to Hassan as having 'a face like a Chinese doll' (p. 3). This is Hosseini's way of referring to Hassan's different ethnicity. Being Hazara, Hassan would have had distinctive facial features, with a flatter nose and narrower eyes than the Pashtuns around him, similar to the Mongolians or the Chinese.

GRADE BOOSTER **A04**

It is important, if you wish to get the best grades, to understand both the internal themes of the book, such as the relationships between fathers and sons, but also the larger external contexts. The history of Afghanistan is complex and turbulent and is key to understanding *The Kite Runner*.

ABSENT MOTHERS

We are also told in this chapter about Amir's mother, Sofia, and Hassan's mother, Sanaubar. The role of women in this novel is largely characterised by their absence, with the lack of mothers and wives making the relationships between Amir, Hassan, Baba and Ali all the stronger. The relevance of the descriptions of Hassan's mother's overt sexuality and her treatment of her husband are revisited later in the story.

STUDY FOCUS: RACE AND HISTORY **A04**

Among the introduction of key characters and the description of childhood events in this chapter, we are given our first insight into the roles of ethnicity and history in the novel. Ali and Hassan are members of the 'Hazara' ethnic group which is seen as being inferior to the 'Pashtun' group of which Amir and his family are a part. We are told about the teasing and taunting of the Hazaras which Amir has witnessed and the book in which he has found records of the persecution and oppression of the Hazaras by the Pashtuns. The fact that Amir finds this information in a book which belonged to his mother, but that its contents are dismissed by his teacher, shows the difference between the way Amir is brought up to view the Hazaras and the way that most Afghanis view them. This is a theme which continues throughout the novel (see **Themes: Religion and ethnicity**).

REVISION FOCUS: TASK 2 **A02** **A04**

How far do you agree with the following statements?

- The way Amir describes his friend makes us like Hassan more than we like Amir.
- *The Kite Runner* is a novel that examines the way the events of history cannot be escaped.

Try writing opening paragraphs for essays based on these discussion points. Set out your arguments clearly.

GLOSSARY

4 **Wazir Akbar Khan** wealthy suburb of Kabul, named after Mohammad Akbar Khan who led a revolt against the British occupation of Afghanistan in 1841

Isfahan a large city in Iran

5 **King Nadir Shah** king of Afghanistan from 1929 until his assassination in 1933

loquat tree an evergreen fruit tree; distant relative of the apple tree

6 **Herati rug** a rug from Herat, a city in western Afghanistan

Allah-u-akbar Arabic for 'God is great/the greatest'

Mashad a large city in Iran

hemorrhaged bled

Istiqlal Arabic for 'independence'

7 **elope** run away, usually to run away to marry in secret

unscrupulous lacking a sense of what is right

congenital a defect or illness present at birth due to inherited or environmental factors

atrophied wasted away from disease or lack of use

bazaar a Middle Eastern street market

naan an Indian flatbread

9 **garrulous** given to talking a lot

Bamiyan the largest town in Hazarajat in central Afghanistan, an important location for Buddhism

CONTEXT **A04**

Ali sings to Amir and Hassan a song about his namesake Ali who was a cousin and son-in-law of the prophet Muhammad, and the cause of the split between Sunni and Shi'a Muslims. The Sunni, the largest branch of Islam, believe that descendants of any of the first four successors to Muhammad (Caliphs) can be seen as legitimate leaders of Islam. The Shi'a, the minority branch of Islam, believe that only those descended from Ali, the fourth Caliph, are the real successors.

CHAPTER 3

SUMMARY

- Amir remembers time spent with his father during his childhood and how his father was disappointed with his lack of manly attributes. Despite this, Amir loved his father very much and was eager for his approval.

- Amir's father, Baba, was seen as a great man by the people around him. He had an ability to achieve more than was expected of him – running a successful business, marrying a beautiful wife and building an orphanage.

- Amir recalls becoming interested in reading and writing as a way to escape his father's lack of interest in him. When he tries to share what he has learnt at school with his father, Baba is scornful.

- Amir comes to believe that his father hates him because he holds him responsible for his mother's death during childbirth.

- Amir overhears his father talking to Rahim Khan about how much more manly Hassan is and that he cannot believe that Amir is his son. Amir then takes out his resentment and jealousy on Hassan.

ANALYSIS

LOVE AND AWE

Amir relates the tale that his father once wrestled a black bear. The nature of this story reinforces the **image** created in the previous chapter of Baba as a strong, powerful man. It also sets the theme for this chapter, which is the love and pride that Amir feels for his father, and also the awe which his reputation creates.

THERE IS ONLY ONE SIN

Baba teaches Amir his own interpretations of scripture: 'there is only one sin, only one. And that is theft. Every other sin is a variation of theft' (p. 16). He explains this comment using the examples of murder being theft of a life and cheating being the theft of fairness. Amir finally understands this and is left with the feeling that he stole the life of his mother by killing her during childbirth. He believes that his father hates him for this.

A MYTHICAL MAN

The story of the building of the orphanage shows that Baba is kind to children, a benefactor and a man of action. However, the way Amir relates the story also highlights the poor relationship between him and his father and his jealousy at the way Baba interacts with Hassan. (This passage is discussed in greater depth in **Extended commentary: Chapter 3**.) Amir continues by telling other stories of Baba's great stature, emphasising his ability to do those things of which other people considered him incapable. In this way, Amir paints his father as an almost mythological figure rather than a real man. His subsequent desire to live up to his father's wishes is therefore revealed as ultimately futile because his goal is a myth rather than a reality.

STUDY FOCUS: LOOKING TO THE FUTURE A01

When Amir confronts his father about his drinking, Baba says of the religious leaders, 'God help us all if Afghanistan ever falls into their hands' (p. 15). This **foreshadows** the later rule of the Taliban in Afghanistan, and injects a note of warning and future tragedy, even at this early point in the story.

SEEKING APPROVAL

Baba and Amir's visit to a Buzkashi tournament emphasises the differences between Amir and his father and also between the boy his father wishes him to be and the boy he really is. Baba's statement that he cannot believe Amir is his son forms a foundation for the story of the relationship between the two, and Amir's striving to make his father proud of him. In the last small section of the chapter we see for the first time how Amir's desire to please Baba turns itself into cruelty to Hassan. Amir identifies this cruelty as evidence of the 'mean streak' (p. 20) Rahim Khan claimed he didn't possess.

CONTEXT A04

Buzkashi (p. 18) is a very popular sport in all of central Asia. The players spend many years learning to master the sport and the specially trained horses are traded for substantial amounts of money.

GLOSSARY

11	**Baluchistan** a region which covers parts of Pakistan, Afghanistan and Iran
12	**Ghargha Lake** a lake near Kabul
	kofta spiced meatballs
	hippies people whose behaviour and dress implies a rejection of conventional values
14	**Farsi** a Persian language spoken in Iran, Afghanistan and Tajikistan
	mullah a Muslim cleric
	hadj an annual pilgrimage to Mecca, the holiest city in Islam
	namaz the Islamic prayer which is performed five times a day
	Koran the Islamic holy book
15	**Genghis Khan** feared emperor of the Mongol Empire in the twelfth century
16	**Kunduz** a city in northern Afghanistan
17	**Khayyám, Hãfez, Rumi and Saadi** Persian poets
18	**aficionado** someone with a passion for and wide knowledge about an activity
	Henry Kissinger Secretary of State in USA, 1973–7, under Richard Nixon's and Gerald Ford's administrations

CONTEXT A04

The principle of *zakat* (p. 14), a custom whereby Muslims are expected to give a specified percentage of their yearly income to charity is the method by which the poor receive welfare in Afghanistan.

KEY QUOTATIONS: CHAPTER 3 A01

Key quotation 1: Talking about his father's impressive abilities, Amir says 'no one ever doubted the veracity of any story about Baba.' (p. 11)

Possible interpretations:

- Suggests that Baba was truly as impressive as Amir tells us he was.
- Shows Amir's great respect for his father, a respect bordering on awe.
- Conveys the possibility that Amir's impression of his father comes from others' reactions to him.

Key quotation 2: Baba tells the young Amir something which he fails to understand. Amir is upset and tells us that 'Baba heaved a sigh of impatience' (p. 16).

Possible interpretations:

- Amir is a lesser man than his father, and so constantly disappoints Baba.
- Amir sees Baba as such a strong man that he cannot help but feel less able.
- Baba cannot empathise with a son who is very different from him and this emerges as disapproval.

EXTENDED COMMENTARY

CHAPTER 3, PP. 12–14

From 'In the late 1960s' to 'hating him a little.'

Although we have already been introduced to the characters of Amir, Hassan and Baba in the first two chapters of the novel, this particular part of Chapter 3 lays out clearly the dynamic between the three characters. The relationships that are outlined here define how the characters interact for the rest of the novel.

The passage takes place first at Lake Ghargha, later the scene of Hassan's dream about the hidden monster, and then at Baba's orphanage. Amir, at this point, is narrating his childhood memories of his father and the building of the orphanage in particular. Amir's **narrative** voice is quite simple, almost childlike, reflecting the perspective of his memories: 'He asked me to fetch Hassan too, but I lied and told him Hassan had the runs. I wanted Baba all to myself' (p. 12). The events related make Baba seem larger than life – as they would to a small child – and aid in the process of mythologising Baba, an attitude which seems to form a large part of Amir's stories about his father throughout the novel.

At the beginning of the passage we are told that Baba has designed the orphanage himself despite having no experience. This shows Baba to be a man who knows his own mind, doesn't listen to discouraging advice, and who is stubborn enough to carry on regardless. This is echoed at the end of the passage where we learn that he had the same attitude to both his business dealings and his marriage. However, it is significant, in terms of Baba's relationship with his son, that Amir identifies himself as the one thing his father had not 'molded … to his liking' (p. 14).

The ability to affect the world around him is a key trait which Amir sees in his father, and many of the anecdotes concerning Baba which Amir relates throughout the novel have this as their main theme. However, the fact that Amir is not malleable in the same way is also always present. During scenes where Baba demonstrates his great abilities, Amir is often shown being unable to live up to his father's wishes.

CHECK THE BOOK **A03**

Orphans and orphanages are recurring **motifs** in *The Kite Runner* and in other literature, including Charles Dickens's *Oliver Twist* (1837–8) and Charlotte Brontë's *Jane Eyre* (1847).

In this particular passage, while Baba is making ready to open the orphanage, we are shown a scene of the two of them having a picnic at the lake. Amir describes himself asking childish questions and making a seemingly random comment about having cancer. This extreme opposition of their behaviour creates a barrier between Amir and Baba: one of the threads running through the novel is Amir's attempts to remove this barrier.

Hassan is not included in the scene which Amir relates, but his absence is key to this passage. Baba has suggested bringing Hassan along with them on their picnic, but Amir has lied to prevent Hassan from coming. Seeing the affection which Baba has for Hassan is hurtful to Amir, and this leads to the cruelty which Amir sometimes shows towards Hassan. This cruelty, submerged in Amir's personality, would seem to be the 'monster' that Hassan later dreams inhabits this lake. However, by preventing Hassan from coming to the lake, Amir can avoid the guilt which he always feels about these cruel episodes. This acts as a **foreshadowing** of Amir driving Hassan away after his rape.

The passage then moves on to the day of the opening of the orphanage and we see Baba once again as an idealised figure. However, as well as Amir's larger-than-life portrayal of his father, we also see other people's reactions to him. This allows us to understand that Baba's charisma and abilities are in fact real rather than simply the romanticised views of his son.

This scene also shows us how proud Amir is of his father. For all that there may be a barrier between the two of them caused by Amir having a very different personality from Baba, Amir still wishes to emulate his father. This contradiction is what powers Amir's story and his journey towards reconciliation with Baba.

During this scene there is a moment when Baba's hat blows off and Amir is asked to hold it for him. The **symbolism** of this moment suggests a self-sufficiency in Baba – he can carry on his speech without needing the support of his hat – and Amir's need to cling on to his father. It also suggests a transference from Baba to Amir: an element of Baba attempting to pass his stature and gravitas to his son. However, Amir is not ready to accept this gift. He can only hold the hat; he is not yet ready to wear it. This is emphasised by the fact that the people who come up to congratulate his father tousle Amir's hair – a symbol of his immaturity and of not yet being ready to assume the mantle of his father. The question that this passage therefore poses is: will he ever be ready?

CHECK THE BOOK **A03**

In his book *The Hero with a Thousand Faces* (1949), Joseph Campbell examines myths for common elements. One which he identifies is 'atonement with the father'. Amir's need to do this is just one of the ways in which his journey matches Campbell's scheme.

CHAPTER 4

SUMMARY

- We learn that Ali, Hassan's father, was an orphan brought up by Baba's father. The two men grew up together, but Amir doesn't remember hearing Baba refer to Ali as a friend.
- When they were growing up, Hassan acted as Amir's servant. Despite this, they spent a lot of time together, with Amir reading stories to the illiterate Hassan. Their favourite story was 'Rostam and Sohrab'.
- After Hassan praises a story that Amir invented, Amir starts writing stories.
- Baba does not wish to read Amir's story, but Rahim Khan does and praises Amir for it. When Hassan points out a possible hole in the plot, Amir becomes angry.

ANALYSIS

CHECK THE BOOK **A03**

The story of Rostam and Sohrab is a tragic tale from the longer epic story, *Shahnameh*, written in the eleventh century by Abolqasem Ferdowsi. It is about a great warrior, Rostam, who defeats and kills his own son in battle, unaware that he is his son.

FRIENDS AND ENEMIES

As Amir relates the story of how Ali came to be his father's servant he draws a comparison with his own relationship with Hassan. He also provides a way of explaining the difference between himself and his father, and Ali and Hassan, on the basis of their religion. The division between their different types of Islam – Baba and Amir are Sunni Muslims, while Ali and Hassan are Shi'a Muslims – makes it hard for them to be true friends.

CONTEXT **A04**

John Wayne (1907–79) was a Hollywood actor who became famous for playing cowboys and soldiers. Whatever role he played, he was always on the side of justice and right.

The films Amir and Hassan go to see at the cinema are mostly Westerns. This is our first mention of the West in the young Amir's story, and again connects us with the older Amir telling the story from his new home in the USA. The **motif** of the Western as a film genre is also relevant, with its clear delineation of good guys and bad guys and justice winning out. Actors like John Wayne can be seen as being similar to Baba in the way Amir looks up to both them and his father as larger-than-life figures.

STUDY FOCUS: THE IMPORTANCE OF SETTING **A04**

We are given rich descriptions of Kabul which evoke the many smells, colours and noises of the city. These not only create a vivid setting for the events of Amir's childhood but also provide a basis for comparison when we are presented with a much-changed Kabul later in the novel. The settings in a novel can be used to reflect mood, plot and character, or to act as a **metaphor** for themes within the text.

THE POWER OF READING

Amir's reading to Hassan seems a friendly and compassionate act, reminiscent of his mother being a teacher. However, Amir does not teach Hassan to read and therefore retains his power over the servant. He is then in a position to use this power against Hassan by teasing him and teaching him the wrong meanings of certain words.

The boys read in an old cemetery under a pomegranate tree. The disused cemetery represents both a place of death, but also, because it is disused, a place beyond both death and life. It is a refuge, a place where the real world cannot reach them. The pomegranate tree, bearing sweet fruits full of seeds, is **symbolic** of life and plenty, but also of the sweetness of the bond between the two boys who share the fruit before Amir reads to Hassan. The cemetery and the tree are symbols which return throughout the novel.

STORIES WITHIN STORIES

Stories themselves are a central motif in the novel. Most of the novel is a story being told to us by Amir, rather than an objective tale being told by a third-party **narrator**. Within that larger story we see Amir read stories to Hassan, such as those of Mullah Nasrudin. At first he adds to and amends them, and finally he moves on to writes his own stories. This creates a bond between him and his dead mother, who was a teacher of literature. However, it also gives him the tools to express feelings which would otherwise be unexpressed. In the first story he writes he creates a scenario which is described by Rahim Khan as **ironic**, but also one which is sad and disturbing. This provides an outlet for his own feelings and a mirror by which we can examine them. In response to Amir's story, Hassan spots a plot hole, showing his ability to see things clearly as opposed to Amir's more muddied and emotional thinking. Amir's 'mean streak' once again appears as he asks himself, '*What does he know, that illiterate Hazara? He'll never be anything but a cook*' (p. 30).

> **CONTEXT** **A04**
>
> Mullah Nasruddin (p. 24) supposedly lived in Turkey in the thirteenth century. Stories of his actions have passed into folklore in a number of countries including Iran, Turkey, Uzbekistan and Afghanistan. He is known as a 'wise fool'.

REVISION FOCUS: TASK 3   **A01** **A04**

How far do you agree with the following statements?

- The use of stories within *The Kite Runner* reminds us that we are reading a work of fiction rather than a true account.
- Understanding the role of religion is key to understanding the whole text.

Try writing opening paragraphs for essays based on these discussion points. Set out your arguments clearly.

GLOSSARY

21	**Zahir Shah**	the last king of Afghanistan, reigning 1933–73
	mast	drunk
	Paghman	a city near Kabul
	contrite	apologetic and seeking forgiveness
	Kandahar	the second largest city in Afghanistan, situated in the south
22	**Agha sahib**	a term of respect, like 'sir'
	Kochi	Afghan nomads
23	*bazarris*	people who browse the stalls in bazaars
	Afghanis	Afghan currency
26	**Chaman**	a town in Pakistan on the border with Afghanistan
27	*Kaka*	a term of familial affection, like 'uncle'
29	*Mashallah*	a quick prayer of thanks to God for an accomplishment
	Inshallah	a phrase translating as 'God willing', expressing hope for a future event

CHAPTER 5

SUMMARY

- Amir and Hassan's conversation is interrupted by a loud roaring noise and the sound of gunfire. These are the sounds of a coup which overthrows the king of Afghanistan.
- Amir and Hassan go to their tree to distract themselves from events. On the way they are attacked by three bullies – Assef, Wali and Kamal – who question Amir about having a Hazara for a friend.
- Hassan scares the bullies off with his slingshot and Assef promises revenge.
- Later, as life returns to normal after the coup, Baba arranges for Hassan's cleft lip to be corrected as a birthday present. Amir informs us, however, in his role as **narrator**, that this was the winter when Hassan stopped smiling.

ANALYSIS

A NEW START

The disturbing noises of the coup are a sign of things changing in Amir's life and, in many different ways, can be seen as the true start of Amir's story with the previous chapters performing the function of introducing the characters and setting the scene. This is the chapter in which the conscious voice of the adult Amir recedes into the background of the story being told. The constant commenting and **foreshadowing** falls away and is replaced by a single **narrative** in the somewhat childlike tones of Amir's younger self.

THE ARRIVAL OF WAR

This is also the chapter in which the traditional Afghanistan of which Amir has been talking starts to change into the modern war-torn country with which we, as readers, are more familiar. Amir comments as the gunfire and explosions sound outside their house: 'They were foreign sounds to us then. … Huddled together in the dining room … none of us had any notion that a way of life had ended' (pp. 31–2). The sounds of the coup are the start of the process which will lead to three decades of war.

THE BULLY

The behaviour of Assef and his friends starts to change Amir's relationship with Hassan. The bullies represent the first real outside threat to Amir's previously comfortable life. Assef introduces himself with an insult containing a sexual swear-word and Amir comments on his previous use of a different word, with similar connotations, as another term of abuse (p. 34). This creates a feeling of sexual threat which always accompanies Assef's role in the novel and foreshadows events to come.

The fact that Amir allows Hassan to stand up for him simply reinforces the impression given in the earlier chapters of Amir's lack of self-confidence and of traditional 'macho' characteristics. It also opens up the gap between Amir and Hassan with Amir's thought, '*he's not my friend! … He's my servant!*' (p. 36), showing how willing he is to sacrifice his friend for his own good.

STUDY FOCUS: USING OUTSIDE REFERENCES — A04

Assef's admiration of Adolf Hitler gives us extra information about how the ruling Pashtun class might view the Hazara people, and also an insight into the extreme character of this bully whom Amir refers to as a 'sociopath' (p. 34). He is representative of the violent, uncaring and self-destructive country which Afghanistan is in the process of becoming at this time. The **connotations** of this reference enable the author to convey a wealth of contextual information in just a few words.

TRYING TO HEAL

By correcting Hassan's cleft lip, Baba reinforces his display of love for the boy and also once more provokes Amir's jealousy. It is a **symbol** of healing and restitution, but is overshadowed by Amir's final comment that the smile that Hassan attempts with his healing lip will be one of his last. Again, this statement foreshadows future events and warns readers that things are about to take a dark turn.

GLOSSARY

31	**staccato**	a musical term for notes which are short in duration and separated from each other
32	**republic**	a system of government with an elected or appointed president rather than an hereditary monarch
33	**brass knuckles**	a hand-held weapon cast of metal with holes for the fingers, used to reinforce the power of a punch
34	**sociopath**	someone who suffers from a personality disorder which causes them to behave in an antisocial and immoral way
	kunis	a term of abuse
36	*quwat*	bravery or conviction
	kasseef	filthy
37	**hierarchy**	a system of levels from greatest to least
38	**constitutional monarchy**	a system of government based on the rule of a monarch
39	*Salaam alaykum*	traditional Arabic greeting meaning 'Peace be upon you'
40	**circumcision**	surgical removal of the foreskin

REVISION FOCUS: TASK 4 — A01

How far do you agree with the following statements?

- *The Kite Runner* is an historical novel.
- Amir is a worse bully than Assef.

Try writing opening paragraphs for essays based on these discussion points. Set out your arguments clearly.

CONTEXT — A04

Hitler and the Nazi regime aimed to rid the world of the Jewish people in what was known as the Final Solution. Similar acts of ethnic cleansing were carried out in Bosnia between 1992 and 1995 and in Rwanda in 1994.

CHECK THE POEM — A03

Amir's description of the sound of the coup with its 'rapid staccato of gunfire' (p. 31) is similar to Wilfred Owen's war poem 'Anthem for Doomed Youth' (1917) where he describes 'the stuttering rifle's rapid rattle' (line 3).

CHAPTER 6

SUMMARY

- In winter the schools close and the children take part in kite-fighting tournaments. Amir and Hassan both enjoy kite fighting.
- When Amir asks for a new kite, Baba buys it for him. However, he also buys the same kite for Hassan which makes Amir jealous.
- When a kite's string has been cut, boys run to catch it. The defeated kites are trophies. Hassan is a gifted kite runner.
- Amir tests Hassan's loyalty by asking him if he would eat dirt if commanded to do so. Hassan says that he would, but challenges Amir over whether he would ever ask him to.
- The 1975 tournament is to be held in Amir's neighbourhood. Amir wants to win to make his father proud.
- The night before the tournament the boys play cards and Amir suspects Hassan is letting him win.

ANALYSIS

A GOOD TEAM

Kite fighting is an activity that Amir and Hassan both enjoy and which enables each of them to excel: Amir at the fighting, Hassan at the running. It brings the two boys together more firmly than any of their other activities and bridges the gulf which Amir sometimes feels between them. It is also an activity of which his father approves and which therefore

provides Amir with a way to secure his father's love and admiration. He describes kites vividly as 'the one paper-thin slice of intersection' (p. 43) between his and his father's otherwise separate spheres.

THE FREEDOM OF FLIGHT

Kite flying is shown as a **symbol** of freedom and of independence. The idea of one kite against many is portrayed as typical of Afghan attitudes. In addition Amir admits that the glass-coated lines would cut his hands but he wouldn't mind. In other situations Amir avoids getting hurt or injured, but this fact shows that for something he truly believes in he is willing to risk getting hurt.

CRITICAL VIEWPOINT **A03**

Kite flying, kite running and kite fighting are topics that recur throughout the novel. These activities can be seen not only to advance the plot but as metaphors for childhood, freedom, war and loss.

CHECK THE POEM **A01**

In 'Kite Poem' (2003), Joyce Carol Oates examines both the thrill and fear of kite flying. It seems an appropriate **metaphor** for Amir's dreams and the fears which hold him back.

STUDY FOCUS: POETIC IMAGERY **A01**

Amir's descriptions of wintertime in Kabul reinforce the feeling of freedom that is suggested by the kites. He uses poetic **imagery** to paint a picture of the city of his childhood: 'The sky is seamless and blue, the snow so white my eyes burn' (p. 42), and he describes 'the soft pattering of snow against my window at night' and 'the way fresh snow crunched under my black rubber boots' (p. 43). By using such language he is able to convey the remembered love he feels for his home city and the beauty which it could achieve in this season.

CHECK THE POEM **A03**

A lively poem describing the joys of winter is Christina Rossetti's 'Winter: My Secret' (1862).

A WIDENING GAP

The conversation between Amir and Hassan about Hassan eating dirt is another sign of the rift that Amir feels between himself and the other boy. It also suggests that Amir is uneasy about placing himself in a superior situation to another human being. He is unsure how to handle this level of power and its responsibilities. Hassan's response, asking 'Would you ever ask me to do such a thing, Amir agha?' (p. 48), shows that he has a clearer understanding of the balance of power between the two of them than Amir does. This is reinforced when Hassan allows Amir to win at cards.

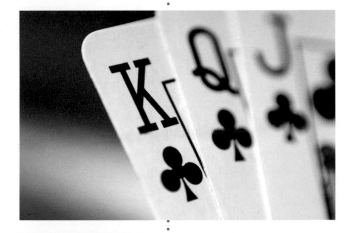

GLOSSARY

42	*qurma*	stew
49	**viable**	capable of surviving/succeeding
50	**panjpar**	a card game

CHECK THE BOOK **A03**

Amir's mistreatment of Hassan, and the guilt he then feels, is similar to how Pip in Dickens's *Great Expectations*, treats his brother-in-law, Joe, after he is informed of his new-found status as a gentleman. Hassan's tolerance and acceptance is also similar to Joe's.

KEY QUOTATIONS: CHAPTER 6 **A01**

Key quotation 1: During a conversation Amir asks Hassan if he would 'Eat dirt if I told you to' (p. 47).

Possible interpretations:

- Amir is testing Hassan's loyalty to him.
- Amir is jealous of Hassan and the thought of forcing the boy to eat dirt pleases him and feeds his growing 'mean streak'.
- 'Eating dirt' is a concept tied up with being at the lowest level in society. By using this image, Amir is showing his awareness of the different social levels he and Hassan inhabit.

Key quotation 2: After Hassan has used the Muslim phrase '*Inshallah*' meaning 'God willing' Amir describes him as 'so goddamn pure, you always felt like a phony around him' (p. 51).

Possible interpretations:

- Amir is jealous of Hassan's depth of belief and is embarrassed that he cannot share it.
- By using the word 'goddamn' Amir shows his disrespect for religion and also reminds the reader of his American identity.
- The word 'phony' can be used to sum up how Amir feels much of the time – like an actor playing a part.

CHAPTER 7

SUMMARY

- The night before the tournament, Hassan dreams that he and Amir are swimming in a lake with a monster in it. They survive their swim and the people watching rename the lake after the boys. In the morning Hassan recounts his dream to Amir.
- Despite being nervous, and with his father watching him, Amir wins the kite-fighting tournament. Hassan runs to catch his kite.
- Amir returns home, but Hassan does not arrive with the kite, so Amir goes out to look for him.
- Hassan is captured by Assef and the other bullies in an alley. Assef offers Hassan his freedom in return for the kite. Hassan refuses.
- The boys rape Hassan while Amir watches, but Amir does not step in to rescue him.
- When Hassan comes out of the alley, Amir takes the kite from him but does not comment on the other boy's distressed state.
- Back home, Amir gets the warm welcome from his father that he has been seeking.

CONTEXT **A04**

The reporting of dreams is a common technique in literature. It can be used as a way of revealing hidden knowledge that characters cannot see for themselves. This idea was examined by the Swiss psychiatrist Carl Jung (1875–1961) in his work on dream interpretation.

ANALYSIS

STUDY FOCUS: THE PIVOTAL POINT **A02**

This is the key chapter of the novel and provides the event on which the rest of the story hangs. The rape of Hassan by Assef is the event that Amir has been **foreshadowing** in earlier chapters and one which he refers back to in future chapters. Many novels feature a central event around which the rest of the **narrative** revolves.

SWEET DREAMS?

The chapter opens with Hassan talking about his dream. In it he and Amir are acclaimed as heroes. This would seem to be a positive omen for the coming kite-fighting tournament. It also demonstrates Hassan's positive state of mind and again reinforces his allegiance with and love of Amir. However, with the image of the lurking monster 'swimming at the bottom, waiting' (p. 52), there is a suggestion that Hassan is conscious of the cruelty which hides beneath Amir's friendly surface and wishes his friend to banish this side of his personality, just as he banishes the monster in the dream.

WINNING AND LOSING

The **juxtaposition** of the tournament and the attack means that the act of winning is immediately contrasted with the act of losing, and the latter is shown to outweigh the former. Upon witnessing the rape Amir is forced to choose between his friend and his father, and by not acting he chooses his father and the praise he will receive for winning the tournament.

At the moment just before the rape, Amir sees Hassan's expression and recognises it as the same look of resignation that the boy wore when Amir was asking him if he would eat dirt if ordered to. In this way Amir draws a direct comparison between what he threatened to do to Hassan and what Assef is actually doing. This makes Amir almost as bad as the bully. During the rape, Amir's narrative breaks off to talk about memories rather than the events actually occurring. This shows the **narrator**'s difficulty in dealing with this part of the story directly, but also the way his mind, as a boy, may have tried to distance himself from what he was seeing.

CONTEXT A04

One of Amir's memories is of the slaughter of a sheep during the festival of Eid-Al-Adha which means the 'festival of sacrifice'.

DARK AND LIGHT

The fact that the rape occurs in an alley is significant. It is not a main street, it is dark, and rarely used, representing the illicit and secret nature of the act. Amir's viewing of the attack is akin to sexual voyeurism and so makes admitting to the event all the harder because he has seen something he shouldn't have been looking at. It also makes it possible for him to dismiss the event because it did not happen in the mainstream of life, but as an aside.

All these events occur on a clear winter's day with the sun shining from a clear blue sky, which Amir refers to before the rape as 'blameless' (p. 53). This makes the winning of the tournament a more glorious event, but makes the rape in the alley all the more dark and disturbing. It is as if the event has dirtied the clean, snow-white day.

GLOSSARY

54	**austere**	stern and cold, morally strict
	morose	overly sad
	chapan	a warm coat or cape worn over the clothes
55	**ayat**	a verse from the Koran
	diniyat class	religion class at school
63	**Bakhshida**	forgiven
67	**demise**	death, ending

REVISION FOCUS: TASK 5 A02

How far do you agree with the following statements?

- The style of writing changes throughout the novel depending on the emotions being felt by Amir.
- The events in the alley make Amir the person he becomes.

Try writing opening paragraphs for essays based on these discussion points. Set out your arguments clearly.

EXTENDED COMMENTARY

CHAPTER 7, PP. 67–9

From 'I stopped watching …' to 'And that was good.'

This passage contains the pivotal events of the novel, which have been **foreshadowed** in previous chapters and which are frequently referenced in later chapters as the source of Amir's guilt and the driving force behind his desire to redeem himself.

The passage opens with Amir looking away from the rape of Hassan which is occurring in the alley. This looking away is mirrored in the way the passage is written. Although it is clear enough to inform the reader of what is happening, it describes the actual attack obliquely, using the sounds and Amir's imaginings and emotions, rather than a graphic description of the rape. Amir tells us that he is 'biting down on [his] fist, hard enough to draw blood from the knuckles [and] weeping' (p. 67). Amir's blood and tears mirror the blood and tears that would be coming from Hassan at the same time but, by focusing on Amir, Hosseini provides an impression of the pain and horror of what is occurring without it being too literal.

Amir then describes the pivotal moment of his life: the decision whether to step into the alley and do something to help his friend, or to run away. He chooses to run away, and the suggestion is that he does not stop running until the end of the novel when he finally makes up for taking the wrong decision at this crucial moment.

The fact that the events are occurring in an alley is symbolic of their hidden and dark nature. Amir's failure to enter the alley shows his inability and unwillingness to deal with the darker side of life and highlights the protected nature of his upbringing up to this point. When he runs away, Amir runs to the bazaar, an open and very public space, taking refuge in a place which represents the safety and shelter to which he is accustomed.

As he runs, Amir tries to rationalise his decision. At first he explains that 'I ran because I was a coward' (p. 68). Then he tries to convince himself that it is not cowardice but self-interest which drives him, and that sacrificing Hassan to placate Assef is the price he has had to pay in order to win Baba's approval: a balancing of fortune for winning the kite fight. This is not a rational thought, based as it is in a superstitious belief, but it shows how Amir's treatment of Hassan is tied up so closely with his desire to gain his father's love. He finishes this thought by dismissing Hassan: 'He was just a Hazara, wasn't he?' (p. 68). This is not typical of Amir who is usually much more open minded about Hassan's ethnicity than the people around him, but it shows not only how ingrained the racism is in the culture, but how much of his own personal belief Amir is willing to set aside in the search for reconciliation with his father.

It is worth remembering at this point that this is not necessarily a true picture of Amir's thoughts at the time because they are being related to us as part of the adult Amir's recollections of the event. As this is the moment that he himself has identified as the critical event in his life it is bound to be coloured by the subsequent thirty years of guilt and constantly running over the event in his mind. The self-recrimination that runs through this passage therefore can be seen as largely that of the adult, not of the child.

Hassan emerges from the alley and Amir confronts him. As he does so he takes a cruel attitude towards him rather than offering care or comfort, asking, 'Where were you? I looked for you?' (p. 68). This anger would seem to stem from Amir's reaction to his guilt and is also an extension of the cruelty he has shown to Hassan from an early age.

At the end of the passage (and chapter), Amir returns home with the precious kite and is greeted by his father with the affection and love for which he has been searching: 'It happened just the way I'd imagined' (p. 69). It would seem that his bargain to exchange Hassan for his father's good regard has come to fruition. Amir is able, for the time of his father's hug, to forget what he has done. However, we know from the preceding dialogue that this moment of respite will be short and the events in that alley will haunt him for many years. We can already see how the gaining of his father's affection will soon be tainted by the bargain which Amir has made to attain it.

CHECK THE BOOK

In the story 'An Encounter' in his collection *Dubliners* (1914), James Joyce also describes a disturbing scene through a voice which is part child and part adult.

CHECK THE BOOK A03

Ian McEwan's *Atonement* (2001) is another novel where the central theme is based on the witnessing of a sexual incident and the lasting effect it has on those involved.

CHAPTER 8

SUMMARY

- After the rape, Amir feels guilty for not having helped Hassan. Hassan retreats to his bed and when Ali asks Amir if anything happened to Hassan, Amir suggests that he is just unwell.
- Baba takes Amir to Jalalabad for the weekend. Amir becomes car sick on the journey, embarrassing his father.
- After Amir returns, Hassan tries to patch up their relationship, but Amir rejects him. Amir's treatment of Hassan becomes more cruel.
- Amir has a birthday party. Assef the bully comes and brings him a biography of Hitler as a present.
- At the party Rahim Khan tells Amir a story about a girl he wanted to marry as an example of how Amir should not let Hassan being a Hazara be a barrier to their friendship. He gives Amir a notebook in which to write his stories.

CHECK THE BOOK **A03**

Rahim Khan's story about the Hazara girl he fell in love with is similar to the story of Shakespeare's *Romeo and Juliet* with its tale of doomed and forbidden love.

ANALYSIS

UNQUIET GUILT

In the aftermath of the rape Amir tries to pretend the events have not occurred. He denies knowing anything and avoids Hassan. He then convinces Baba to take him away from the house without bringing Hassan, literally distancing himself from his problems. Amir's later request that his father get rid of the servants is a further example of him trying to distance himself from his guilt, this time by removing them from his home. The car sickness and insomnia he suffers from are other ways in which Amir feels he appears weak to Baba. With no outward expression, Amir's guilt has become something physical.

COMPLICITY

Amir's realisation that he was the monster in Hassan's dream has a self-pitying and melodramatic tone to it as he tells us 'he'd been wrong about that. There was a monster in the lake. … I was that monster' (p. 75). Thus we start to see how Amir views his guilt and illness as a deserved punishment for his lack of ability to help Hassan, just as his poor relationship with his father is his punishment for his having 'killed' his mother during his birth.

Likewise, the presence of Assef and his family at the birthday party creates a feeling of a shadow falling across the occasion. The spectre of Hitler is once more raised in Assef's gift. By giving the book about Hitler to Amir, a symbolic link is made again between Assef's bullying and Amir's refusal to help. The final vision is of Assef bullying Hassan at the party and Amir once more unable to bring himself to stop it, reinforcing this idea.

STUDY FOCUS: SYMBOLISM **A02**

Amir's and Hassan's return to their usual spot under the pomegranate tree is significant: this location is no longer the refuge from the world it used to be because Amir brings his feelings of guilt with him. In a replay of the 'eating dirt' scene, which has already been compared in Amir's mind to the moment of rape, Amir attacks Hassan with the pomegranates which used to be a **symbol** of their bond, thus finalising the breaking of the bond. By reacting as he does, hitting himself with a final pomegranate, Hassan once more shows the acceptance which Amir saw on his face at the time of the rape and refuses to let Amir assuage his guilt by fighting back.

GLOSSARY

72	*Khala*	a familiar term of affection, similar to 'Aunt'
74	**lamb kabob**	spiced lamb often cooked on a stick
	tandoor	a clay oven
75	**insomniac**	a person who is unable to sleep
86	*pari*	fairy or angel

KEY QUOTATIONS: CHAPTER 8 **A01**

Key quotation 1: When Amir tells his father that Hassan is unwell, Baba looks worried. Amir says he 'couldn't help hating the way his brow furrowed with worry' (p. 71).

Possible interpretations:

- This demonstrates, once again, Amir's jealousy over Baba's feelings for Hassan.
- Later, when we learn Baba is Hassan's father, this expression of worry makes sense to us.
- Amir's use of the word 'hate' can be seen to be associated with his father as well as Hassan because he resents his strong desire to please his father.

Key quotation 2: At his own birthday party, Amir nearly tells Rahim Khan about witnessing the attack on Hassan, but he stops himself. He wonders what Rahim Khan would think of him and concludes, 'He'd hate me, and rightfully' (p. 87).

Possible interpretations:

- Fear of other people's reactions is what prevents Amir from telling them what he witnessed.
- Rahim Khan's opinion of Amir is as important to him as Baba's opinion.
- As readers we suspect that Rahim Khan would not have the reaction that Amir fears. In this way we can see that it is actually Amir who hates himself, rather than it coming from others.

REVISION FOCUS: TASK 6 **A02**

How far do you agree with the following statements?

- The message of *The Kite Runner* is that it is better to tell the truth than keep secrets.
- The novel demonstrates that our natures are formed by the people around us.

Try writing opening paragraphs for essays based on these discussion points. Set out your arguments clearly.

CONTEXT **A04**

According to the Koran, pomegranates are one of the fruits that Muslims will find in the garden of paradise; they are supposed to be a cure for envy and hatred.

CONTEXT **A04**

Hassan's refusal to fight back when Amir attacks him is similar to the Christian idea of 'turning the other cheek' (Matthew 5.38–41). This theme also exists in Islam in the thirty-second of the Forty Hadith of an-Nawawi: 'There should be neither harming nor reciprocating harm.'

CHAPTER 9

SUMMARY

- For Amir's birthday, Hassan and Ali give him a new copy of the book Amir used to read to Hassan.
- Amir plants a watch that he received for his birthday under Hassan's mattress, then goes to his father and falsely accuses Hassan of stealing birthday presents.
- When asked about this by Baba, Hassan admits the theft. Amir is shocked and realises that Hassan knows he saw the attack in the alley.
- Baba forgives Hassan, despite his earlier statements about theft. However, Ali and Hassan still decide to leave. Baba pleads with them to stay, something Amir has never seen his father do before.
- Amir watches Ali and Hassan leave. It is raining and he imagines a scene from a film where he would run after the car and all would be forgiven, but he does not act on this.

ANALYSIS

WAGES OF SIN

Amir opens his presents but, as with the time he spends alone with his father in the previous chapter and even his possession of the kite at the end of the tournament, he takes no pleasure in them. His guilt over what happened to Hassan, and his failure to do anything to help, overshadow any joy he might get from the gifts. He sees them as the profits of his sins rather than as a reward for doing well in the tournament and as such does not feel he deserves them. The concept that he invokes of them being 'blood money' (p. 89) is reflected most keenly in the fact that the bike his father gives him is a rich, red colour.

IMPORTANCE OF BOOKS

There are only two presents which mean anything to him. The notebook Rahim Khan gives him is a reward for his writing rather than his kite flying and so is not sullied by the events of Hassan's rape. It is also **symbolic** of the one ability which makes Amir an individual, his ability to write. The second significant present, the storybook chosen by Hassan, also has these connections but it acts as a reminder of what he has lost by his cowardly actions. This provokes Amir's guilt and converts it into action, leading to his subsequent framing of Hassan for the theft of his other presents.

The gift from Hassan of a new copy of the *Shahnamah* is not merely symbolic of the boy's friendship, but also has a deeper significance. The title of the book translates as 'The Book of Kings' and recalls Amir's carving of 'Amir and Hassan, the sultans of Kabul' (p. 24) into the pomegranate tree, as well as Hassan's remembrance of the phrase in his dream before the kite-fighting tournament.

CHECK THE POEM **A03**

The concept of gifts or earnings being tainted by the actions of the receiver, as expressed by the term 'blood money' (p. 89), refers to the pieces of silver paid to Judas Iscariot for betraying Jesus. This image is used by Walt Whitman in his 1850 poem 'Blood Money', which attacks a fugitive-slave law.

TOO LATE

While the incident with the pomegranate was a straightforward attempt by Amir to relieve his guilt by allowing Hassan to take revenge on him, Amir's planting of his supposedly 'stolen' birthday presents under Hassan's mattress is an attempt to remove his guilt by removing its cause. It is also the next step in his attempt to put distance between himself and Hassan. This time he is successful, but the fact of Ali and Hassan leaving makes Amir finally realise that he should have been honest about what he saw. He imagines how, in a film, he would 'chase the car, screaming for it to stop … pull Hassan out of the backseat and tell him [he] was sorry, so sorry' (p. 94). However, this realisation comes too late and Amir is left with his guilty secret and the knowledge that his father was willing to forgive Hassan for the theft, thus demonstrating again a remarkable level of affection for his servant's son.

Another key moment in this chapter is Amir's realisation that Ali finally knows what has happened to his son and Amir's role in the affair. However, he reflects the attitude of his son and does not say anything to Baba, protecting Amir but also refusing to relieve him of his guilt.

> **CRITICAL VIEWPOINT** A03
>
> Amir hiding his watch and money under Hassan's mattress could be seen as a **motif** as it is repeated later in the text when he revisits Afghanistan. On this second occasion, however, he is motivated by charity.

STUDY FOCUS: PATHETIC FALLACY A01

The departure of Ali and Hassan causes Baba to cry, something which we would not expect from the character already presented to us. This is then reflected in another moment of **pathetic fallacy** in the rain storm which accompanies their departure. Amir tells us that summer rain was rare, just as his father's tears were rare. Amir himself does not cry, but the rain instead provides symbolic tears through which to view this event.

GLOSSARY

88	**Polaroid**	a camera which takes photos which develop instantly
	transistor radio	a small portable radio
93	**rickshaws**	small carts for carrying people usually pulled by other people
94	*raka'ts*	the sections of the ritual Islamic prayers

REVISION FOCUS: TASK 7 A03

How far do you agree with the following statements?

● The novel demonstrates that stories reflect the world back to us.

● A compelling story must include examples of both good and evil.

Try writing opening paragraphs for essays based on these discussion points. Set out your arguments clearly.

CHAPTER 10

SUMMARY

- It is 1981 and Amir and his father are escaping from Russian-controlled Afghanistan. They stop so Amir can be sick, and he remembers all that they have had to abandon.
- They are stopped at a roadblock and Baba stands up to a Russian soldier who is threatening to rape a female Afghan refugee. Baba is nearly shot, but the soldier is reined in by his commander.
- They arrive in Jalalabad but the truck which is meant to take them out of the country is broken. They have to stay in the basement of a house with similarly stranded refugees.
- They finally make the last part of their journey in an empty fuel tanker. One of the bullies from the attack in the alley, Kamal, who is also escaping, dies on the journey and his father kills himself.

ANALYSIS

INTO THE FUTURE

The action moves abruptly forward in time by five years from the moment of the departure of Ali and Hassan to the flight of Baba and Amir from Afghanistan. Amir is now eighteen years old. By this time the country was occupied by Russian troops and many people chose to emigrate and leave everything behind rather than continue to live in what had become a very dangerous country.

STRONG FATHER, WEAK SON

Amir is struck with car sickness during their escape, once more revealing his weakness in front of his father and embarrassing him. This is contrasted with the scene of Baba showing his strength and bravery by preventing the Russian soldier from raping the woman in the truck. This moment also acts as a contrast with Amir's actions in the alley where he did not prevent the rape of Hassan.

THE RUSSIANS IN AFGHANISTAN

The Russian soldier who wishes to rape the woman is singing an Afghan wedding song as he approaches the truck. This shows how much the Russians have become part of Afghan life, but also how little respect they have for the Afghans themselves that he should sing such a song and then attempt such an action.

CONTEXT A04

The Soviet army entered Afghanistan in 1979 to oppose groups of Afghan Mujahedin rebels and started a war which lasted until 1989. Many Afghans fled the country and found sanctuary in places like Pakistan and, due to the anti-Soviet sentiments of the Cold War, the USA.

CHECK THE FILM A03

The 2007 film *Charlie Wilson's War*, starring Tom Hanks, examines the way in which the US government funded the Mujahedin rebels in the war against the Soviet and Afghan communists.

CONTEXT A04

'Ahesta Bero', the song which the Russian soldier sings, is often sung at Afghan, Iranian and Tajik weddings to accompany the entrance of the bride and groom, much as Richard Wagner's 'Bridal Chorus' (often called 'The Wedding March') is used in Christian ceremonies.

STUDY FOCUS: CONTRASTS **A02**

After Baba saves the woman from rape, her husband kneels and kisses Baba's hand. This demonstrates, as with Amir's previous tales of his father, the regard that other Afghans have for Baba, regardless of the circumstances. It also shows a culture of respect that is absent from the driver of the truck who has taken their money to pay for the escape. In these two actions we see the traditional Afghanistan, where there is a spirit of community and mutual respect, and the new Afghanistan, which is a land of unrest, exploitation and personal struggle. Contrasting ideas placed together form a **juxtaposition**, where the contrast points out important issues.

DARK DESCENT

There is a vivid description of the basement in which Amir and his father wait for the final part of their journey. Amir describes how he can see 'shapes huddled around the room, their silhouettes thrown on the walls by the dim light of a pair of kerosene lamps', and later, 'I discovered the source of the scratching sounds. Rats' (p. 104). In this short passage a claustrophobic environment is laid out in stark contrast to Amir's earlier descriptions of the house Baba built for them. It demonstrates the change in their status which their flight from Afghanistan has caused. This is extended in the change into the present tense for the description of the interior of the oil tanker in which they make the final leg of the journey.

However, despite its initial horror, the death of Kamal on the escape from Afghanistan can be seen as **symbolic** of a chance for Amir to escape his problems and the potential for him to move on with his life in a new country, without bringing all of the 'baggage' of his past with him.

CHECK THE POEM **A03**

The Khyber Pass through which Amir and his father pass to reach Pakistan has long been identified as a natural border between Russian-held lands and the Indian sub-continent, as in Rudyard Kipling's poem, 'The Ballad of the King's Jest' (1890).

GLOSSARY

97	*Shorawi*	Soviets
	Peshawar	large city in northern Pakistan
98	*rafiqs*	companions
	Poleh-charkhi	Afghan prison
	Kalashnikov	a Russian rifle
99	**MiG**	Russian fighter-plane
	Spasseba	Russian for 'thank you'
100	**negate**	cancel out
101	*Roussi*	Russians
107	*rubab*	a stringed instrument similar to a guitar
	encapsulated	expressed in brief terms, summed up

CHAPTER 11

CONTEXT A04

The parts of the novel set in and around San Jose and San Francisco reflect Khaled Hosseini's own life. Having left Afghanistan, his family settled in San Jose in 1980, and it was here that Hosseini attended high school, college and medical school.

SUMMARY

- It is the 1980s and Amir and Baba are now living in California, in the USA. Baba likes the strength of America, but the pollution and lack of fresh foods make him ill.

- Baba refuses to learn English or adapt to his new country but is still capable of commanding respect amongst ex-pat Afghans.

- Amir graduates from high school and decides to study English and creative writing at college. His father wants him to study something that will lead to a 'proper job' but Amir stands his ground.

- Baba and Amir buy items from garage sales and sell them from a stall in the Afghan section of the San Jose flea market.

- Amir falls in love with a girl named Soraya, the daughter of an Afghan general, whom he meets at the flea market.

ANALYSIS

CHECK THE BOOK A03

The central section of *The Kite Runner* is set in an Afghan community in California. In this it is similar to other **post-colonial** novels such as Zadie Smith's *White Teeth* (2000) and Monica Ali's *Brick Lane* (2003), which show the experiences of emigrants.

AMERICAN PRIDE

This chapter echoes the events of Chapter 3 in which Amir describes his father's reputation. Once again he outlines events which demonstrate Baba's pride and the stature which he has in his community. However, these are all now set in an American context and these attributes are viewed slightly differently. Amir is seen to fit in better in America than his father, placating the grocery clerk and graduating from high school. However, Baba's natural ability to gain the respect of others is shown to be as potent in this new country when he becomes the new best friend of the customers in the bar where they go to celebrate Amir's graduation.

A SMALL PIECE OF THE PAST

Baba's trading of small items in the San Jose market is also a reflection of the tale told in Chapter 3 of Baba becoming a successful merchant against the odds. Again it is in a new context, one in which Baba is a newly arrived immigrant, but it shows a continuation of the same spirit and also, from Amir's **narrative** of these events, that he still holds his father in the same regard. Being a part of the flea market in San Jose is also a way for Baba to hold onto his heritage. He trades within the Afghan part of the market and knows many of the people there from Afghanistan. In this way he is able to retain a small piece of what he has left behind.

STUDY FOCUS: SEEING IN REFLECTION — A02

In this chapter Amir meets Soraya. She, like Amir, is the child of an influential, powerful and well-regarded man. She is also a beautiful young woman who makes an instant impression on Amir. Baba's comment on Soraya's past, that 'a few days, sometimes even a single day, can change the course of a whole lifetime' (pp. 123–4) is key here. It a sentiment to which Amir can relate, and the suggestion is that it forms a significant part of his attraction to her. She acts as a mirror, reflecting Amir's own life back to him.

GLOSSARY

110 **Jimmy Carter** 39th president of the USA, 1977–81

Leonid Brezhnev Soviet premier, 1964–82

Ronald Reagan 40th president of the USA, 1981–9

ESL English as a second language

Amtrak American railway system

116 **Hayward** a city in California, near to San Francisco

tashakor – thank you

117 *khanum* literally 'queen', a courteous title for a woman

chatti a term of derision

KEY QUOTATIONS: CHAPTER 11 — A01

Key quotation 1: Introducing their move to the USA, Amir says that 'Baba loved the *idea* of America' (p. 109).

Possible interpretations:

● The quotation shows that, like Amir, Baba is quite westernised.

● The italics used for the word 'idea' show us that while Baba might like the things America stands for, he does not feel the same way about the reality of the place.

● This is a seemingly positive statement, but the emphasis on 'idea' warns us that problems will emerge.

Key quotation 2: Amir describes America as, 'Someplace with no ghosts, no memories, and no sins.' (p. 119)

Possible interpretations:

● The USA would seem to be an ideal place for Amir as, if this description is true, it will allow him to escape the guilt from his past.

● An objective view of America would suggest that this description is not true and, as a result we are led to question Amir's truthfulness as a narrator.

● The fact that Amir sees the USA in this way suggests that he is again ignoring his problems rather than facing up to them.

REVISION FOCUS: TASK 8 — A02 A03

How far do you agree with the following statements?

● The novel suggests that the past should never be forgotten.

● Love is the most important emotion in *The Kite Runner*.

Try writing opening paragraphs for essays based on these discussion points. Set out your arguments clearly.

CONTEXT — A04

Soraya Taheri is one of the few female characters in the novel, and certainly the most prominent. She shares the name Soraya with a former queen of Afghanistan, the wife of King Amanullah Khan and an early and powerful champion of women's rights in Afghanistan.

CONTEXT — A04

Baba's graduation present to Amir is a Ford Gran Torino (mis-named a 'Grand Torino' in the novel). This was the car used in the television series *Starsky and Hutch*. It is a reminder of the Ford Mustang Baba owned in Kabul, which was the car driven by Steve McQueen in the 1968 film *Bullitt*. This ties in with Amir's love of American films and culture.

CHAPTER 12

SUMMARY

- Amir is in love with Soraya and spends time with her at the flea market, talking about stories and books.
- Amir's attentions are welcomed by the girl's mother, but he is warned off by her father.
- Baba falls ill with lung cancer. He refuses to accept treatment and forbids Amir from telling anyone about his illness.
- After Baba collapses at the flea market and is rushed to hospital, Amir asks him to approach Soraya's family for her hand in marriage, and it is all agreed.
- Soraya reveals to Amir that she ran away from home when younger and lived with a man. Amir wishes he could tell her his own guilty secret, but is unable to do so.

ANALYSIS

LYRICAL LOVE

Amir opens the chapter as he ended the previous one, by describing his feelings for Soraya. In both instances his use of descriptive language comes to the fore once again. He talks about 'the shadow her hair cast on the ground when it slid off her back and hung down like a velvet curtain' (pp. 125–6) and calls her '[t]he morning sun to my *yelda*' (p. 126). He explains that *yelda*, the first night of winter, was a night when animals and insects searched for the lost sun, but was also the night of lovers' vigils. For him, every weeknight becomes *yelda* as he waits to see Soraya at the Sunday market. This poetic language recalls the style used when introducing Hassan and when describing Kabul in winter. It is associated with the most important things in Amir's life, and shows the high level of regard in which he holds Soraya.

STUDY FOCUS: THE POWER OF EDUCATION A04

During one of her conversations with Amir, Soraya explains how she taught the servant they had in their house back in Afghanistan to read. This contrasts with Amir's refusal to teach Hassan and, in fact, with his teasing of him for being illiterate and the way he would teach him the wrong meanings of words he didn't know. Amir sees in Soraya both echoes of his mother but also a reflection of the version of himself that he wishes he could have been. Soraya is also a symbol of the old, pre-Taliban Afghanistan, before education for women was banned.

THE WEIGHT OF THE PAST

Soraya's mother is much more welcoming to Amir than Soraya's father. This is not a sign that she is any less a traditional Afghan than her husband but more an indication of how desperate she is for any young man to pay attention to her daughter, due to Soraya's history. Again, the fear that no one will want her daughter because she has been with another man stems from a traditional Afghan view of marriage. Amir's willingness to overlook this fact is partly due to his Americanisation but also his reluctance to condemn another for the sins in their past because of the continuing weight of his guilt over Hassan.

In contrast to Amir's happiness at being in the USA, Baba has not adapted so well. To that extent his illness can be seen as a reaction to being there, or rather to not being in Afghanistan. There is an element of 'pining' in the way he wastes away. However, the host of people who visit him in hospital is a sign that the regard of others has not diminished.

CRITICAL VIEWPOINT A02

During the descriptions of Baba's illness, Amir uses technical language associated with the treatment of cancer. This replaces the use of Farsi and Pashtun words in earlier chapters, suggesting that these medical terms are the hidden language of America, which for Baba is a place of sickness.

GLOSSARY

126	*ahmaq*	fool
127	*mozahem*	an intruder
	Khoda hafez	goodbye, literally 'God, safe'
128	*lochak*	a swindler
	mohtaram	repected
130	*ahesta boro*	Afghan bridal music
	henna	a paste used for temporary tattoos
131	**chaperoning**	accompanying young unmarried people to ensure nothing improper occurs
133	*bachem*	my child
134	**pulmonary**	relating to the heart
135	**CAT scan**	a medical scan which produces a 3-D image of the inside of the body-part scanned
136	**bronchoscopy**	an examination procedure that involves inserting a small camera into the airways
	prognosis	prediction of the course of an illness
	chemotherapy	treatment using chemicals, usually a term used when treating cancers
	palliative	treating of the symptoms rather than curing the disease
138	*Komak!*	Help!
	911	emergency telephone number in the USA (999 in the UK)
139	**metastasized**	spread
140	**oncologist**	doctor specialising in cancer
141	*Balay*	yes

REVISION FOCUS: TASK 9   A02

How far do you agree with the following statements?

● The novel suggests that our ability to learn is what separates mankind from animals.

● Amir's experiences demonstrate that home is where you choose to make it.

Try writing opening paragraphs for essays based on these discussion points. Set out your arguments clearly.

CHAPTER 13

SUMMARY

- Amir is engaged to Soraya. The engagement period is cut short because of Baba's health. On his wedding day, Amir thinks about Rahim Khan and Hassan.

- Soraya moves in with Amir to help to look after Baba. One day Amir discovers she has been sharing his stories with Baba. This moves Amir to tears.

- A month after the wedding Baba dies. The funeral reminds Amir of his father's stature in Kabul, and how much he relies on his father's strength.

- Amir learns that Soraya's father, the General, suffers from migraines and still hopes to return to Afghanistan. Her mother has suffered a stroke and now worries about her health.

- Amir secures a place at college and later has his first novel published.

- Amir and Soraya try to have children but are unable to do so.

CHECK THE BOOK A03

In *The Kabul Beauty School* (2007), Deborah Rodriguez describes having visited post-9/11 Afghanistan with the aim of connecting with the country's women. Among other topics she looks closely at the various intricacies of Afghan wedding ceremonies.

ANALYSIS

A WEDDING

Amir and Soraya's courting and subsequent marriage ceremony are both very traditional, if shortened because of Baba's illness. This would seem to be Amir's final attempt to make his father proud of him and to show Baba that he can be a true Afghan.

The recurrence, during the ceremony, of the Afghan wedding song which was sung by the Russian guard during Baba and Amir's escape from Afghanistan is a demonstration of the safety of the USA compared to Russian-occupied Afghanistan, but also a sign of continuity, of bringing the old country into the new. It shows Amir finally starting to grow into his heritage. The reappearance of this song also suggests that the past cannot be escaped. Thus when Amir and Soraya look at each other in the mirror, one of the most intimate moments of the ceremony, Amir is wondering about Hassan and 'whose face he [Hassan] had seen in the mirror under the veil? Whose henna-painted hands had he held?' (p. 149).

CHECK THE POEM A03

Rumi, a thirteenth-century Persian poet listed as one of those Amir studied at school, wrote a number of poems sometimes read at modern Persian weddings, including 'Wedding Bliss', 'Words for a Wedding' and 'Our Feast, Our Wedding'.

A FUNERAL

Baba's death follows quickly after the wedding. Baba is finally able to relinquish hold on life because he has seen his son become a man and knows that he will be taken care of. Baba's reading of Amir's stories at least partly lays to rest Amir's constant need to make his father proud of him. However, at the funeral, Amir realises how large a figure in his life his father has been and how large a gap is left to fill.

FAILURE TO THRIVE

The general's migraines and Jamila's hypochondria are, like Baba's cancer, signs of the ill effect that living in the USA has on that generation of Afghans. As Amir gets to know his new parents-in-law better, we can see that he does not hold them in the same esteem as he held Baba.

STUDY FOCUS: SUCCESS AND FAILURE **A04**

In contrast to Soraya's parents, both Soraya and Amir are happy and healthy. However, their mysterious infertility can be seen as another example of the Afghans not being able to thrive away from their own country. The revelation of their infertility is coupled with the news of Amir getting his first two novels published. As with the story of the tournament and Hassan's rape it would seem as though Amir has had to trade one success – his potential fatherhood – for another – the publishing deal. In addition, Amir's success is shown in contrast to a change in the fate of Afghanistan, from Russian occupation to civil war and infighting, suggesting that Amir's success is also at Afghanistan's expense. This contrast shows the differences between the prosperous USA and the war-torn Afghanistan, making it more significant when Amir decides to return to Kabul.

GLOSSARY

145	*ghazal*	love song
	Ustad Sarahang	Afghan musician
147	*noor*	light
149	*sholeh-goshti*	flame-cooked meat
	attan	Afghan dance
153	*chila*	wedding ring
154	**raga**	Indian musical form
155	**maladies**	illnesses
160	**Merlot**	a red wine

160 *Mujahedin* a Muslim who is engaged in a holy war – used to refer to those who fought against the Soviets in Afghanistan

Najibullah the fourth and last president of the communist Democratic Republic of Afghanistan

Tiananmen Square large, open square in Beijing, China; site of prominent protests in 1989

161 *Kho dega!* So!

alahoo God

nawasa grandchild

CONTEXT **A04**

A migraine usually involves a combination of headache and nausea and, very often, a sensitivity to light. There are thought to be a number of different causes, although it has been found that genes can play a part in a person's likelihood of suffering from migraines. In adults it is a condition which afflicts far more women than men.

CONTEXT **A04**

As Amir publishes his first book, the Soviet armies pull out of Afghanistan. This occurred in response to the collapse of the Soviet Union, the fall of the Berlin Wall and the end of the Cold War. However, rather than allowing the Afghans to re-establish peace, leaders of the militias established themselves as warlords with their own areas of control, and civil war continued.

CHAPTER 14

SUMMARY

- The story returns to June 2001 and Amir receives the phone call from Rahim Khan who is sick and wants Amir to come to Pakistan.
- Rahim Khan's message, '*There is a way to be good again*' (p. 168), tells Amir that the older man has always known about the events in the alley.
- Amir and Soraya are still childless. They rarely speak of this, but it is clearly a problem in their marriage.
- Soraya arranges for her parents to stay with her while Amir is away. Then Amir flies to Pakistan.

ANALYSIS

A SECRET REVEALED

The revelation that Rahim Khan has known about the secret Amir has been holding all these years is a powerful one. We already know from previous chapters that Hassan's rape weighs heavily on Amir and that he has tried, on a number of occasions, to find a way to atone for his actions on that day. Finally, with this phone call from Rahim Khan, Amir is being offered a way to 'be good again' (p. 168).

STUDY FOCUS: A BALANCED STRUCTURE **A02**

Analysing the structure of a text can give you a way to understand its complexities. This chapter marks the mid-point of the novel both in terms of the content and the plot. It brings the story up to date with the events mentioned in Chapter 1 and finishes Amir's relation of his history. The story from here covers events after Rahim Khan's phone call in June 2001 from the perspective of Amir talking to us in December 2001: a period of six months.

PAYING A DEBT

Amir's and Soraya's childlessness remains a factor in their lives. This information is coupled with Amir dreaming of Hassan. The **juxtaposition** of these two passages suggests that Amir cannot have children of his own until his debt to Hassan has been paid and his guilt finally assuaged. The memories of Hassan's friendship and loyalty demonstrated by the repetition of the phrase '*For you, a thousand times over!*' (p. 169) thus lends added poignancy to what Amir describes as the 'futility' (p. 169) of the act of lovemaking he has just performed with his wife.

REVISION FOCUS: TASK 10 **A02** **A04**

How far do you agree with the following statements?

- Rahim Khan's call gives meaning to Amir's life.
- *The Kite Runner* demonstrates that forgiveness is important.

Try writing opening paragraphs for essays based on these discussion points. Set out your arguments clearly.

CHAPTER 15

SUMMARY

- Amir arrives in Peshawar in Pakistan and meets a very ill Rahim Khan. This is the first time Amir has seen his old friend since he and Baba left Kabul.

- Rahim Khan recounts to Amir the terrible changes in Afghanistan and the brutality of the Taliban regime. He goes on to say that he is dying and wants Amir to perform a final favour for him. He then tells Amir about Hassan who lived on in Baba's old house with Rahim Khan after Amir and Baba had left.

ANALYSIS

A SECOND LOSS

The last time Amir and Rahim Khan spoke was over the death of Amir's father, Baba. Many times in the novel Amir comments on how he might have preferred to have Rahim Khan as his father, and now he finds this surrogate father is also dying. These deaths precipitate the changes in Amir from a scared boy into a strong man. To some extent, the death of Rahim Khan will be more significant, because he not only was a clearer guide for the young Amir, but also he knows Amir's secret and so can provide the means to overcome it.

STUDY FOCUS: THE PART STANDS FOR THE WHOLE   A01

The destruction of Baba's orphanage represents a **symbolic** second death of Amir's father and also can be as seen as a personal affront. The orphanage was a symbol for Amir of his father's strength and compassion. The death of children is also a personal tragedy for a man who remains childless. This is just one of the many instances in *The Kite Runner* where children are either threatened or actually hurt, their vulnerability forming a recurrent **motif** which does much to represent the breakdown of culture and family in Afghanistan over the period covered by the novel. This is also an example of **synecdoche**, a technique where a part of a thing is used to represent the whole thing (such as saying 'Nice wheels!' when referring to the whole car).

THE WAY TO BE GOOD AGAIN

The end of this chapter sees the return of Hassan to the story as a character rather than just a symbol of Amir's guilt. Amir's decision to listen to the story of Hassan, which he admits to himself he does not want to hear, shows the opening up of his mind to the possibilities of change and redemption. Having declined the chances he had at the time, he is finally taking advantage of an opportunity to make things right.

GLOSSARY

170	**Jamrud** a town on the edge of the Kyber Pass
	Cantonment a semi-permanent military quarters or residential barracks
173	**INS** Immigration and Naturalization Service, a US government agency
	Ghazi Stadium sports stadium in Kabul named after Sardar Shah Mahmud Khan Ghazi, prime minister of Afghanistan from May 1946 to 7 September 1953
174	**Deh-Mazang** town near Kabul
175	**caracul** a type of coarse wool

CONTEXT   A04

Peshawar is a large city in Pakistan, close to the border with Afghanistan. At times in its history it was part of the Afghan empire and still has a large Afghan population. It was the first destination of most Afghans fleeing the Soviet invasion.

CRITICAL VIEWPOINT   A03

The descriptions of Peshawar as a city 'bursting with sounds', '[r]ich scents, both pleasant and not so pleasant', with 'carpet vendors, kabob stalls, [and] kids with dirt-caked hands selling cigarettes' (p. 171) remind the reader of earlier descriptions of the Kabul of Amir's childhood.

CHAPTER 16

SUMMARY

- Rahim Khan relates the story of what has happened to him since Amir last saw him.
- Unable to maintain Baba's house by himself, Rahim Khan seeks out Ali and Hassan to help him.
- He travels to a village just outside Bamiyan where he finds Hassan, who tells him that Ali was killed by a landmine.
- Rahim Khan asks Hassan and his wife, Farzana, to live with him. Hassan at first refuses, but agrees after learning of Baba's death.
- Farzana gives birth to a stillborn baby, but then later becomes pregnant again. Shortly afterwards, Hassan's mother, Sanaubar, returns to the house, starving and ill.
- Hassan and his wife nurse his mother back to health. She in turn delivers Farzana's son, Sohrab. Sanaubar dies when Sohrab is four.
- Hassan tries to give his son a normal life, despite the turmoil in the country. This becomes more difficult in 1996 when the Taliban take over the country.

ANALYSIS

MULTIPLE VOICES

This is the only chapter in the novel not to be told from Amir's perspective. Although it is still written as a **first-person narrative**, it is the voice of Rahim Khan that we hear. This voice is different in tone and in sentence construction from Amir's voice, which points up the particular style of Amir's passages. Phrases such as 'Allah forgive me' (p. 178) and the use of the word 'would' in sentences such as 'I would take a walk', 'I would pray *namaz*' or 'I would rise in the morning' (p. 178) suggest a more considered and thoughtful voice than Amir's.

A CHANCE TO START OVER

Just as Rahim Khan is Amir's surrogate father and the man who holds the key to his redemption, so Baba was a second father to Hassan. Hassan's return to Kabul on the news of Baba's death reflects Amir's return to Pakistan because of Rahim Khan's illness. Both men see a chance to regain what they lost as children at the point at which they lose the support of their father figures.

STUDY FOCUS: GENDER ISSUES   A01

In Rahim Khan's story we discover that Hassan has married and we also see the return of his mother, Sanaubar. Women have been largely absent from the novel, and feature mostly at moments of change. The mothers of both Hassan and Amir leave the **narrative** shortly after giving birth. Soraya enters the story as Baba is dying and Sanaubar only re-enters the story after Hassan has returned to Kabul following the deaths of Ali and Baba. Even so, this remains a male-centred narrative as we see when Hassan's daughter is stillborn but his son, Sohrab, survives.

CONTEXT   A04

Bamiyan is the largest town in Hazarajat. It was made famous by the ancient giant statues known as the Buddhas of Bamiyan which were carved into a mountainside there. These were destroyed by the Taliban in 2001.

CONTEXT   A04

Landmines were the favoured weapon of the Mujahedin during their conflict with the Soviets, and were often planted on their behalf by children.

CHECK THE BOOK   A03

In *Swallows of Kabul* (2004), Yasmina Khadra explores in greater depth the events in Afghanistan which Rahim Khan relates in this chapter.

CHECK THE BOOK   A03

The Kite Runner is largely a novel about men and their relationships in the absence of women. As a counterbalance to this, Hosseini's second novel, *A Thousand Splendid Suns* (2007), concentrates on the experience of women in Afghanistan over the same time period.

STORYBOOK SON

Hassan's son's name is taken from the storybook which Amir used to read to Hassan. This is another example of the importance of stories in the novel but also looks back to a happier past and is another example of Hassan's enduring loyalty to Amir. Rahim Khan describes the young boy as an avid reader, like Amir, but also a talented kite runner and slingshot shooter like Hassan. With these two attributes it seems as though Sohrab is being described as the son of both Hassan and Amir; the son Amir has failed to have and the fulfilment of the potential which Amir's actions denied Hassan.

BUILDING DEFENCES

Hassan's rebuilding of the 'Wall of Ailing Corn' (p. 183) is **symbolic** of trying to rebuild what he used to have, as well as building a boundary between the haven that is Baba's house and the war in the outside world. The banning of kite fighting is a symbolic destruction of the happier remains of Amir's past – and the massacre of the Hazaras in Mazar-i-Sharif. This final event demonstrates how the prejudice against the Hazaras which was evident during Amir's childhood – especially in the attitudes of Assef and his friends, but also in those of ordinary people – has become engrained at a higher level and has now led to violence and murder.

> **CONTEXT** **A04**
>
> In the summer of 1997 the Taliban attempted to occupy the town of Mazar-i-Sharif, a Shi'a stronghold, but failed. They returned in August 1998 and massacred many Hazaras and other local people.

GLOSSARY

178	*chai*	spiced tea
180	*Arg*	a large Persian citadel
183	*burqa*	a traditional item of Muslim clothing for women of this area, which covers the head, face and body
185	*isfand*	plant burned to create smoke to ward off bad luck
	Sasa	grandmother

REVISION FOCUS: TASK 11   A02

How far do you agree with the following statements?

- *The Kite Runner* is actually a novel about children.
- The absence of female characters in the novel is as important as the presence of so many male ones.

Try writing opening paragraphs for essays based on these discussion points. Set out your arguments clearly.

CHAPTER 17

CONTEXT   **A04**

The decades of war in Afghanistan and the brutal regime of the Taliban left a large number of orphans who have become the focus of aid organisations from all over the world. Providing food and shelter for them all is a huge problem.

SUMMARY

- After hearing Rahim Khan's story, Amir asks if Hassan is still living in the house. Rahim Khan gives Amir a photograph of Hassan and Sohrab and a letter in which Hassan says he would like to see Amir again.
- Rahim Khan reveals, however, that Hassan and his wife were murdered by the Taliban a month after the letter was written. Their son, Sohrab, is now living in an orphanage in Kabul.
- Rahim Khan asks Amir to go to Kabul and find Sohrab. He also tells him that Baba was Hassan's real father, making Hassan Amir's half-brother. Amir is angry at never knowing this and storms from the apartment.

ANALYSIS

A PERSONAL MESSAGE

The photograph of Hassan allows his story to be brought up to date, with a physical representation of him in adulthood. Hassan's letter, as with Rahim Khan's story, gives us a separate voice from Amir's with a different style of speech. For example the opening 'In the name of Allah the most beneficent, the most merciful, Amir agha, with my deepest respects' (p. 189) is a much more formal and intricate way of writing than we see from Amir. This mode of communication finally allows Hassan to reveal his love for and loyalty to Amir in his own voice, rather than simply from Amir's interpretation.

HOME AND AWAY

In Hassan's letter he touches on many of the same things we have heard about in Amir's story. This verifies that these things – the cemetery, the pomegranate tree, the storybook – were as significant to Hassan as Amir has claimed. He also brings our story of Kabul up to date and highlights the differences between what they experienced in their childhood and how life is now. Hassan stayed behind and has grown and changed with his country. Amir, in contrast, having left in 1981 is in a state of suspended animation with his development as an Afghan stunted at an early age.

AN AFFECTING DEATH

The death of Hassan affects Amir at least as profoundly as the death of his father and the news of Rahim Khan's illness. As at other moments of stress in the novel, the structure of the language breaks down and Amir can utter nothing more than denials, attempting to hold back his emotions about the loss he is feeling – both in terms of Hassan's death but also in terms of his chance for atonement. It means that he can now never seek forgiveness from Hassan for what he did as a child. However, as with the death and illness of the other two main influences in his life, this is another spur forcing Amir towards maturity and towards accepting his inheritance.

STUDY FOCUS: AMIR'S QUEST   A02

Rahim Khan's request that Amir go to Kabul and rescue Sohrab is Amir's chance to finally do penance for failing Hassan. The fact that the boy is in an orphanage is a reference back to Baba's orphanage. Saving Sohrab is presented as something Baba would have done and something that will enable Amir to become the man his father wished him to be, as well as repay his debt to Hassan. This is a 'quest', a common plot element in mythology, where characters set off to achieve or find something in order to gain a reward.

CHECK THE POEM   A03

Illegitimacy has been a common theme of literature, even as far back as Robert Burns's poem, 'Address to an Illegitimate Child' (1785) and beyond.

BLOOD BROTHER

In the final part of this chapter, the web of responsibilities between Baba, Amir, Hassan and Sohrab is made all the clearer when Rahim Khan reveals that Hassan was Baba's illegitimate son, and therefore Amir's half-brother. This information about Hassan's parentage refers back to the conversations about bloodlines in Chapter 13 and the importance to Afghans of knowing who their parents and ancestors are. It is this attachment which Rahim Khan hopes will convince Amir to do as he is asked.

GLOSSARY

188	**Urdu**	official language of Pakistan
192	**herringbone vest**	a waistcoat made of black and white thread in a zigzag pattern

CHAPTER 18

SUMMARY

- Amir considers the news that Hassan was his half-brother and realises that it explains Baba's affection for the boy.
- He considers the possibility that if he had not betrayed Hassan, Ali and his son may now be still alive in the USA.
- Amir realises that he has no choice but to go to Kabul to find his nephew.

ANALYSIS

FATHER-SON SECRETS

As Amir walks the streets trying to understand the fact that Hassan was actually his brother he realises that he is not so different from his father: 'As it turned out, Baba and I were more alike that I'd ever known' (p. 197). They both had a secret with regard to their Hazara servants. In Amir's case it was the betrayal of Hassan by not helping him during his rape; for Baba it was the knowledge that he had slept with Ali's wife and was Hassan's father.

However, Amir realises that he denied his responsibility to Hassan while Baba did his best to make amends by taking care of both Ali and his son and trying to treat Hassan as kindly as he treated Amir. Amir now understands the reasons behind Baba's fondness for Hassan, the way he would treat both boys equally, the offence he took when Amir wanted to get new servants and the sorrow he felt when Ali and Hassan left.

CONTEXT **A04**

Lollywood (p. 196), the term coined for the Pakistan film industry, based in Lahore (hence the leading 'L'), produces films in a number of languages, including Pashto, making the Pashtun-dominated Afghanistan a key export market.

KEY QUOTATIONS: CHAPTER 18   A01

Key quotation 1: Having learned that Baba was Hassan's father, Amir remembers Baba's lesson that lying was the same as stealing, and that stealing was the worst sin. He thinks, 'fifteen years after I'd buried him, I was learning that Baba had been a thief' (p. 197).

Possible interpretations:

- Despite fifteen years having passed, Amir is still so caught up in his image of his father as a perfect man that a single failing feels like a betrayal.

- Amir is upset because this new knowledge has revealed his father to be less than the 'ideal man' he had imagined him to be.

- Amir's indignation is misplaced. He himself has kept secrets and, even worse, betrayed his friend.

Key quotation 2: Thinking of Baba's actions, Amir realises his own offences and thinks, 'like father, like son' (p. 197).

Possible interpretations:

- Amir refers to this phrase as a cliché, which it is, but it is not one that Amir has previously felt able to apply to himself as he always saw himself as so different from his father.

- The phrase is used dismissively, to cast both Amir and Baba as bad men who wronged their friends. However, by the end of the novel, Amir will also have acquired some of Baba's better attributes.

- Amir is disappointed to find that his father is just a man, like him.

CHECK THE FILM   A03

The 2002 film *Road to Perdition*, starring Tom Hanks, also examines how the relationship between a father and son is strained by the revelation of secrets.

REVISION FOCUS: TASK 12   A03 A04

How far do you agree with the following statements?

- The novel suggests that secrets should always be revealed.

- *The Kite Runner* is a novel about cities.

Try writing opening paragraphs for essays based on these discussion points. Set out your arguments clearly.

CHAPTER 19

SUMMARY

- Amir returns to Taliban-held Afghanistan to rescue Sohrab. On the way he suffers a recurrence of his car sickness.

- Once back in Afghanistan, Amir feels out of place – like a visitor. Farid, the driver who has helped Amir enter the country, accuses Amir of always having been a visitor in his own country.

- Farid takes Amir to stay with his brother Wahid. Wahid asks why he has returned and Amir explains about Sohrab.

- Wahid says he is proud to have Amir stay in his house and gives him all the food he and his family have to eat. Farid is ashamed of his earlier accusations.

- Farid agrees to help Amir with his mission now that he realises the reason for his return. Before they leave, Amir hides a handful of money under his mattress to repay the family for their kindness.

ANALYSIS

HARSH REALITY

The stories of Rahim Khan and Hassan may have informed Amir about the state of Afghanistan, but he is still shocked and saddened by what he sees. This is the country he abandoned, and his feelings for it have been bound up with his feelings about his relationships with both Baba and Hassan. Seeing the country in this state is like seeing his internal landscape ravaged by all the years of guilt. This is an association Amir makes clear when he comments, 'My mother had died on this soil. And on this soil, I had fought for my father's love' (p. 210).

A NERVOUS RETURN

Once again Amir is car sick while being driven to Jalalabad. This sickness seems to be caused, at least in part, by the country itself because we are only told about him being sick when travelling through Afghanistan. It is a continued sign of his weakness: the reaction that he has to his own country ties in with Farid's comments about him being a tourist in his own land. (This issue is discussed further in **Extended commentary: Chapter 19**.)

However, the welcome Amir receives from Wahid and his family is in contrast to Farid's initial suspicion of Amir's motives for returning. Wahid's reaction is representative of traditional Afghan hospitality proving that it still remains in the country despite the decades of war. Farid is a product of the new Afghanistan and is reminiscent of the cynical Karim, the truck driver who helped Baba and Amir escape from the country in the first place.

> **CRITICAL VIEWPOINT** (A03)
>
> The concept of *watan* (homeland) is strong throughout the text. Notice how Amir's sense of home shifts as the story progresses.

STUDY FOCUS: BEGINNING TO ATONE (A02)

Despite Wahid's welcome being warm and traditionally generous, the fact that making Amir welcome leaves no food for the rest of the family shows how difficult it is for Wahid to maintain his traditional values during such impoverished times. Upon realising that he has eaten all Wahid's food, Amir feels guilty, but it is a sign that he has not yet achieved the stature of his father that he does not approach Wahid with his gift of money but instead hides it under a mattress. As Amir comments, this is the same method he used to disgrace Hassan so many years ago. As a symbol, leaving the money for a good purpose shows the penance which Amir is trying to perform; however, it could also be suggested that it shows a continued level of cowardice and a refusal to face up to matters. It does, however, show that he has completed the first stage of his quest for atonement.

GLOSSARY

201	**Hindu Kush**	mountain range separating Pakistan and Afghanistan
	Tajik	someone from Tajikistan
202	**jihad**	struggle or effort
	Shari'a	Muslim legal system
	ruminate	to think over
	rationalize	to provide reasons for a course of action
203	***mehmanis***	parties
205	**dilapidated**	falling apart from age and misuse
	adobe	building material made from sand, clay, water, straw and sometimes dung
206	***hijab***	headscarf, sometimes with attached veil

REVISION FOCUS: TASK 13 (A02)

How far do you agree with the following statements?

- The state of Afghanistan on Amir's return is **symbolic** of his feelings over the deaths of Baba and Hassan.
- Amir's car sickness is psychological, i.e. all in his head.

Try writing opening paragraphs for essays based on these discussion points. Set out your arguments clearly.

EXTENDED COMMENTARY

CHAPTER 19, PP. 203–4

From 'We had crossed the border' to 'alongside the road'.

This passage does two things. It gives us a shorthand description of the state of Afghanistan at the time of Amir's visit, and it also emphasises the great extent to which Amir's need to re-engage with his nationality and ethnicity form part of his journey.

The first paragraph is a description of what Amir sees from his car window. It echoes the strongly **imagistic** language which has been used elsewhere to describe the significant things in Amir's life. In this case, the images focus on the destruction and desolation of the country, making the description all the more effective. As well as describing the current state of Afghanistan, the paragraph also deals with the history which has brought the country to its current state. First we are shown the poor housing, much of which is seemingly uninhabitable, damaged by fighting. Nearby there are children 'dressed in rags' (p. 203). The people are living in extreme poverty: their houses destroyed and their clothing in tatters.

The next image is of a group of men sitting on 'an old burned-out Soviet-tank' (p. 203). This brings in the Soviet invasion and the wars of the late 1970s and 1980s. However, because we are told that the tank is now only a relic, we know that this is just another part of the story which has led to the scenes of poverty and devastation. Behind the men is a woman dressed in a burqa. This is a specifically Islamic garment which covers the woman's entire body and, in Afghanistan, all of the face except the eyes. The fact that the woman is wearing this particular item represents the regime of the Taliban and their oppression of the Afghan people, and thus the completion of the story that Amir sees from his car window.

Amir's reaction to these sights is to express his feeling of alienation from his country and his people by comparing himself to a visitor. He says to Farid, 'I feel like a tourist in my own country' (p. 203). The use of the word 'tourist' shows the extent of the distance he feels, because a tourist is a person who visits places for fun and generally has no interaction with the indigenous people, as opposed to a traveller or other type of visitor.

Farid picks up on this word and accuses Amir of having always been a tourist in Afghanistan. He goes on to surmise a background for Amir which is remarkably close to the truth and lays bare just how protected Amir has always been from the realities of life in Afghanistan. This confirms that the picture Amir has painted of the Afghanistan of his youth was of a privileged family, rather than a typical one. The suggestion is that Amir has never really understood what it means to be an Afghan because he has been insulated from the reality by his father.

Farid's reaction to Amir in this passage is not representative of the welcome which Amir receives in his home country and is in sharp contrast to the attitude of Wahid, Farid's brother, later in the chapter. However, it would seem to represent the underlying thoughts of at least some of the Afghans who remained behind during the troubles, and suggests that a greater level of cynicism has become standard in the ordinary citizens.

Amir reacts to Farid's verbal attack with a bout of car sickness. This is once again a sign of his weakness and inability to cope with the pressures of life. It is a measure of how unlike his father he is. However, coming hard on the heels of the revelation regarding Amir's protected status, it suggests that his weakness is a reaction to his having been overprotected. At the points when the real world impinges on him, Amir becomes ill. Facing this will be the final step on Amir's journey to maturity

CHECK THE POEM A03

The term 'tourist' can indicate someone who watches events without taking responsibility. Paul Engle explores this idea in his poem entitled 'Tourist' (*A Woman Unashamed and Other Poems* (1965)).

CONTEXT A04

Motion sickness is usually caused by a difference between the amount of movement detected by the eyes and by the inner ear. This often leads to nausea and vomiting. Amir's sickness, however, is probably caused by some form of anxiety attack.

CHAPTER 20

SUMMARY

- Amir is shocked by the state of Afghanistan. On arriving in Kabul he discovers it has been severely damaged by twenty years of war.
- The Taliban patrol the streets looking for people to punish. Amir is advised to avoid even looking at them.
- They meet a beggar who was formerly a university lecturer working alongside Amir's mother. The beggar gives them directions to the orphanage where they hope to find Sohrab.
- Amir arrives at the orphanage and, after some argument, discovers that Sohrab has been sold by the director to a prominent member of the Taliban. Amir questions this activity and learns that it is the only way the man can fund the care of the remaining children.
- The director tells them they will find the man who bought Sohrab at the next day's football match.

ANALYSIS

RUBBLE AND RUIN

Amir continues his education about the real state of his home country. Kabul is even more damaged than he could have imagined. The city that formed the backdrop to all his childhood memories is almost unrecognisable. By revisiting this city and re-educating himself – seeing it, as he says, 'through Farid's eyes' (p. 213) – he is bringing himself closer to what remains of his Afghan heritage. He uses rich **imagery** to describe this new version of Kabul in order to evoke the pain and sadness he feels at what he sees. He describes children playing amongst 'jagged stumps of brick and stone' (p. 215), recalling the time when he used to play in the city himself, and talks about the city as an old friend who is now 'homeless and destitute' (p. 216). This contrasts with his descriptions of the city he remembers from his childhood and, in doing so, suggests the trauma of seeing the city in such a state.

UNREAL

Upon arriving in the city he sees the Taliban in the flesh for the first time. While everyone else looks away, Amir stares at them. This reinforces Farid's earlier comment about Amir being a tourist in his own country. He watches the Taliban as if they were an item on the news. He still cannot entirely connect with the reality of the situation in his country.

CHECK THE BOOK **A03**

In *The Bookseller of Kabul* (2003), Asne Seierstad provides a vivid picture of life in Kabul under the Taliban and in the years since.

STUDY FOCUS: COINCIDENCE A02

The technique of coincidental meetings is a common one in literature and allows the author to give structure to the story. The appearance of the beggar seems a remarkable coincidence but is, as with Wahid's generosity, a sign of the old Afghanistan still existing despite the terrible conditions and the wars of the previous three decades. It is also a **symbol** of how little regard the Taliban have for education and the tragedy of modern Afghanistan where educated men are reduced to begging.

THE CHILDREN'S PRICE

With Baba's orphanage having been destroyed, Sohrab has been kept in a converted warehouse in one of the most badly damaged parts of the city. It is an unsuitable building and the children are kept in rooms with 'no floor covering but matted carpets and windows shuttered with sheets of plastic' (p. 222). As with the news of the original orphanage having been destroyed, this is a personal affront to a man who so dearly wants children and cannot have them. Increasingly the state of Afghanistan seems to be part of Amir's divine punishment both for his offences against Hassan but also for deserting Afghanistan. With no people like Baba and his offspring to provide and protect the country and its inhabitants, Afghanistan has been left as vulnerable and fatherless as its orphans. The director's tales of the Taliban's crimes and his own compromised morality are simply extensions of this idea.

GLOSSARY

214	**tabla**	a type of drum
222	*yateem*	orphans

REVISION FOCUS: TASK 14 A02

How far do you agree with the following statements?

● Even though he is an adult when he returns to Afghanistan, Amir is still essentially a child.

● The events in this section of the novel suggest that the people of Afghanistan have become used to the rule of the Taliban.

Try writing opening paragraphs for essays based on these discussion points. Set out your arguments clearly.

CONTEXT A04

Kabul University was established in 1931, but was almost completely closed during the rule of the Taliban. It has since started to function once more as a university, and is being rebuilt and restaffed.

CHECK THE FILM A03

In *Slumdog Millionaire* (2008) children of the Mumbai slums in India are 'rescued' and employed as beggars by a corrupt orphanage owner.

CHAPTER 21

SUMMARY

- Amir returns to his old neighbourhood. It is largely undamaged because it has been taken over by the new leaders, though it has not been maintained well.
- Amir climbs the hill to the old cemetery and discovers that the pomegranate tree has died. However, the inscription that he had carved into the trunk still remains.
- Amir and Farid check into a hotel and Amir finds that things like the food and the humour are still unchanged. However, he also finds familiarity in Farid's expression of casual prejudice about the Shi'a.
- Amir and Farid watch the man in sunglasses – the man who bought Sohrab from the orphanage – stone two people to death at a football match. Farid makes arrangements for Amir to meet the man.

ANALYSIS

REVISITING THE OLD

Amir finds that his old neighbourhood is largely unchanged because the Taliban have chosen this as the area in which to settle. This reinforces Farid's earlier comments about Amir's privileged upbringing. If the place where he grew up is considered the preferred place by those who could choose any part of the city, then it shows how impressive a part of the town it is.

Amir stares at his house for a long time, longer than Farid is comfortable with. This is part of the process Amir is going through, reconnecting with the childhood he has been running away from all his life. He now realises that he no longer wants to forget the past but to embrace it and move forward. This is a demonstrable step in his healing process.

STUDY FOCUS: PROGRESSION   A02

One of the features of **narrative** is that elements change as it progresses. Amir arrives at the pomegranate tree out of breath, 'each ragged breath … like inhaling fire' (p. 230), showing how he is an older person than the one who used to come up here. He also finds that the tree is now dead. The tree was a **symbol** of the close relationship between Amir and Hassan, so its death symbolises the end of that relationship as brought about by Hassan's death. However, the inscription that Amir carved, with his and Hassan's names, is still there, showing that their friendship can exist beyond the barrier of death.

CRUEL SPORT

The spectacle of the stoning taking place in the middle of the football match finally brings home to Amir the situation he is in and the state of his homeland. The fact that the man he needs to meet is the one doing the stoning makes it all the more real. The **juxtaposition** of these two events suggests that the stoning would be seen in the same light as the football – as a sport – and the crowd's reactions reinforce this idea as they watch and shout comments. The suggestion is that the Afghan people have become used to the violence and now view it as an ordinary occurrence. Amir reports that the 'crowd made a startled "OH!" sound' (p. 237) during the stoning, but nothing more. Only Amir has any strong reaction, hiding his face and waiting for it to be over. It is a naive and childlike response, connecting back to the Amir whose development as an Afghan stopped when he was still a child and who, unlike those who stayed behind, has not been desensitised to the constant violence. This continues the theme of the return journey being Amir's chance to finally grow up and reminds us that he is still struggling to do so.

HYPOCRISY

The Talib who does the stoning is dressed all in white and wearing John Lennon-style sunglasses. This is **ironic** as white is a symbol of peace and purity – attributes which are at odds with the man's actions. In addition, the sunglasses are symbolic of a decadent Western consumer society, but are being worn by a member of a religion which bans all such things. In this way, the Talib is shown as a hypocritical figure as well as a cruel one. The reference to John Lennon suggests that this man has the status of a rock star within Afghanistan.

GLOSSARY

228	**semilunar**	half-moon shaped
229	**Rorschach inkblot**	random shapes used by psychologists to provoke unconscious reactions to help diagnose patients
231	*azan*	Islamic call to prayer
	mueszzin	the person at the mosque who performs the call to prayer
232	**Panjsher Valley**	a region of Afghanistan in the north
237	**John Lennon sunglasses**	small round sunglasses such as those worn by John Lennon of the pop group The Beatles

CONTEXT **A04**

Death by stoning was the usual punishment for adultery under the Taliban. Despite the ending of their regime and the passing of equality laws, the practice of stoning women to death, for a variety of reasons, has continued in some regions.

CHAPTER 22

SUMMARY

- Amir, wearing a false beard to blend in, goes to a large house in his old neighbourhood to meet the man in sunglasses who has bought Sohrab. As he enters, he passes men with rifles, and wonders if he will survive the encounter.

- The man appears, covered in the blood from the stoning, and removes Amir's disguise. He taunts him with references to the stoning and the massacre at Mazir.

- The man accuses Amir of treason for having left Afghanistan, then sends for Sohrab. The boy, who looks remarkably like his father, is forced to dance for them.

- The man shows that he knows Amir's identity and then reveals himself to be Assef, the bully from Amir's childhood. He asks why Amir wants the boy, but Amir refuses to tell him.

- Eventually Assef gives Sohrab to Amir, but tells him that the price he must pay for the boy is to finish their childhood fight.

- Assef fights with Amir and hurts him badly, but Amir is saved by Sohrab who, like his father, uses a slingshot and incapacitates Assef. Amir and the boy escape with Farid.

ANALYSIS

BECOMING THE FATHER

This chapter sees Amir badly frightened at the situation he finds himself in but finally standing up and emulating both his father's and Hassan's acts of bravery. His journey of self-discovery has finally brought him to a confrontation with his own childhood fears in the form of the bully, Assef, who is now a leading Talib.

It seems appropriate that Assef has risen to this position of authority. In a country where social norms have broken down, it is likely that those in power behave as sociopaths. Assef is clearly in his element and fulfilling a role for which he was always suited. He has finally found a way to emulate the man he earlier declared as a hero, Adolf Hitler.

REPEATING THE PAST

When Sohrab enters the room Amir once more comments on how much the boy looks like his father. This acts as a reminder to Amir of the attack which Assef perpetrated against Hassan, and so spurs him on. By fighting Assef in order to save Sohrab he can also fight to save Hassan and repay his debt to his former servant. In describing the boy, Amir repeats some of the descriptive language he used to first describe Hassan. He mentions the 'Chinese doll face of my childhood' (p. 244), but the contextual language is harder and less poetic, reflecting the harsh circumstances in which he is encountering Sohrab.

> **CRITICAL VIEWPOINT** **A02**
>
> Consider the theme of recurrence and repeating history in *The Kite Runner*. The event in which Sohrab defeats Assef with a slingshot is just one of many which could be seen as tying the past and present together.

STUDY FOCUS: SUBVERTING IMAGES A01

One way of making an impact in writing is to change, challenge or undermine common images. Upon first meeting Assef, Amir notices that there is blood on his white clothes from the stoning. This alters the **symbolism** of these clothes from purity and peace, to being like a butcher's apron. There is also the **image** of blood on white sheets associated with the loss of virginity, suggesting that by engaging in the fight with Assef, Amir is losing the last of his innocence and naivety.

THE PAIN OF REDEMPTION

By going through with the fight, Amir is at last able to lay his demons to rest and, just as Assef started to laugh when a beating helped him pass an excruciatingly painful kidney stone, so Amir starts to laugh as the beating he receives from Assef finally banishes the pain and guilt he has felt ever since Hassan's rape. It is the beating he has felt he deserved ever since that day and which he tried to provoke from Hassan by throwing pomegranates at him.

Amir is once more rescued by a boy with a slingshot in a scene which harks back to the first aborted fight between Amir and Assef. However, in this case, Amir has taken full part in the fight and has no reason to be ashamed. Sohrab then fires the slingshot and performs the action that his father threatened Assef with all those years ago. This ends a battle which started in Chapter 5, showing the circular nature of the **narrative**.

> **CHECK THE POEM** A03
>
> 'The child is father of the man' is a line from the poem 'My Heart Leaps Up When I Behold' (1802) by William Wordsworth. It means that our childhood experiences shape the adult we grow up to be.

GLOSSARY

244	***rupia***	Indian currency
	pirhan tumban	traditional Afghan dress
245	***dil-roba***	an Indian stringed instrument
248	**kidney stones**	small stones of calcium which can form in the kidney and cause acute pain while being passed from the body
253	***Bas***	enough
254	**vitreous fluid**	thick liquid inside the eyeball
	Bia	come (with me)

REVISION FOCUS: TASK 15 A02

How far do you agree with the following statements?

- The novel suggests that great change requires great suffering.
- Assef has been as successful, in his own way, as Amir.

Try writing opening paragraphs for essays based on these discussion points. Set out your arguments clearly.

CHAPTER 23

SUMMARY

- Amir is in hospital after his beating, having suffered severe injuries. He has a dream, in which his father wrestles the black bear before turning into Amir.
- Rahim Khan has gone away to die in peace. He leaves a letter forgiving Amir for his childhood mistakes. He explains that Baba was hard on Amir because he could not openly show his love for Hassan.
- Farid searches, but discovers no sign of the adoptive parents Rahim Khan promised for Sohrab.
- Amir decides to take Sohrab with him to Islamabad while he considers what to do.

ANALYSIS

ASSUMING THE MANTLE

When Amir dreams of wrestling the bear we can see how he has finally achieved, in his own mind at least, the stature of his father. By standing up to Assef, Amir has found a way to be the man his father always wanted him to be. Amir's split lip shows that, from his battle, he has come to resemble Hassan, his half-brother, making them almost like twins. This is a very physical sign that Amir has been able to repay his debts to Hassan.

Rahim Khan's letter is his final communication and the sign of his death. With Amir having achieved his growth into a man it is fitting that the last part of his childhood is sloughed off. In the letter Khan confirms what Amir has already been thinking about with regard to his father's guilt over the fathering of Hassan.

STUDY FOCUS: A BATTLE A02

In mythology, quest stories end with a large battle – such as the one in the previous chapter between Amir and Assef – in which the **protagonist** overcomes not only the foe, but often his own weaknesses or inadequacies. The hero emerges with a prize, which may be something physical, or something internal such as self-respect or understanding. So, when Farid uses the phrase 'For you a thousand times over' (p. 266), echoing Hassan, it not only demonstrates the loyalty that Farid now feels for Amir, but also shows that this is a loyalty which Amir has earned through his actions. On the journey from Peshawar to Islamabad, which occurs at the end of this chapter, Amir is not reported to suffer from car sickness. It seems that, in facing his childhood fears and overcoming them, he has cured this weakness as well.

GLOSSARY

256   **Clark Gable**   American actor from the first half of the twentieth century, famous for his well-trimmed, thin moustache

259   **hemorrhage**   bleed

       splenectomy   operation to remove the spleen

       pneumothorax   air trapped next to a lung

260   *Al hamdullellah!*   Praise to God

262   *shalwar-kameez*   traditional Asian dress comprising a long top hanging over trousers

270   **hodgepodge**   mixture

CHAPTER 24

SUMMARY

- Sohrab goes missing in Islamabad, but Amir finds him near the Shah Faisal Mosque. They talk about Hassan and Sohrab tells Amir that the Taliban men 'did things' (p. 278) to him of which he is ashamed. Amir invites Sohrab to return to the USA with him.

- Amir explains to Sohrab that he is the boy's uncle. Sohrab is scared that Amir might place him in another orphanage. Amir promises that this won't happen.

- Amir calls Soraya who is happy for him to bring Sohrab home. Amir discovers that the process of adoption is very difficult and admits to Sohrab that he may have to go into an orphanage for a time.

- Soraya tells Amir to bring the boy home and complete the paperwork in the USA. Amir goes to tell Sohrab but is shocked by what he finds.

ANALYSIS

THE SAFETY OF RELIGION

The fact that Sohrab runs to a mosque is a sign that Hassan brought him up as a good Muslim, but also that he does not associate his fear of the Taliban with the mosque. For Sohrab, it seems, the Taliban are not associated with his religion.

A NEW IDENTITY

Amir's panic at finding Sohrab missing suggests that this is probably the first time he has had to be truly responsible for someone else. It indicates a new chapter in his life and is underlined by the manager of the hotel agreeing to help him because he is 'a father like you' (p. 275). When the manager leaves Amir outside the mosque he says to him that 'you people [Afghans] are a little reckless' (p. 275). This makes Amir laugh, partly because he has always been cautious. It is also a sign that he has finally accepted his Afghan identity.

STUDY FOCUS: A REWARD **A02**

The mythical structure of the book continues with Amir receiving his reward at the end of his quest. Amir's decision to take Sohrab to the USA with him is the final stage in his change from the Amir who arrived in Pakistan. He has paid his debts and is now ready to be a father. If all the bad things that have happened to him and to Afghanistan can be seen as his punishment for his sins, then now, having repented and been forgiven for them, he receives a reward: the son he has always wanted. Although the path will not be a straightforward one – Amir is forced to admit he might have to break his promise to Sohrab – Amir keeps trying and through Soraya is provided with a simple solution.

GLOSSARY

276	*masjid*	mosque
279	*Pakeeza*	Indian film of 1972
282	*Haddith*	teachings of the prophet Muhammad
283	*tashweesh*	worry
298	*Rawsti*	anyway, after all

CONTEXT **A04**

The Shah Faisal Mosque is one of the largest mosques in the world. It is about 5,000 square metres in area and can hold over a quarter of a million worshippers.

CONTEXT **A04**

The INS was the United States Immigration and Naturalization Service. It was responsible for legal and illegal immigration and naturalisation until 1 March 2003 when its functions were taken over by the Department of Homeland Security.

CHECK THE BOOK **A03**

'Javert' (p. 286) is the name of the police inspector in Victor Hugo's novel *Les Misérables* (1862). This is also a novel in which much of the **narrative** is driven by the main character seeking redemption for past mistakes.

CHAPTER 25

SUMMARY

- Sohrab has attempted suicide in the bath. Amir attempts to pray for both Sohrab and Hassan.
- The boy survives but is uncommunicative and withdrawn. When Amir reads to him from a storybook, Sohrab wishes for the return of his old life or for death.
- Amir takes Sohrab back to the USA, but the boy's depression doesn't lift.
- When Soraya's parents meet Sohrab the General makes a dismissive comment about this 'Hazara boy' (p. 315). Amir challenges this racism and reveals Sohrab's – and Hassan's – parentage.
- Months pass in which the events of 11 September 2001 occur and Amir and Soraya become involved in projects to end the years of war and unhappiness in their homeland.
- The novel ends in the same park where it began. Sohrab helps Amir to fly a kite in a kite fight. This finally rekindles the boy's spirit and Amir adopts the role of the kite runner.

CONTEXT A04

The events of 11 September 2001 triggered the NATO-led invasion of Afghanistan and the overthrow of the Taliban.

ANALYSIS

THE FINAL RECONNECTION

As Amir waits for Sohrab to be treated following his suicide attempt, and during his recovery, the process whereby Sohrab has become fused in his mind with Hassan comes to an end. Amir has now totally accepted Sohrab as his kin, his responsibility, even as his son. He starts to pray, something which has not been important to him for a long time, but which is important to Sohrab. The survival of Sohrab comes immediately after Amir's prayers, suggesting that these prayers have been answered and that there will be a continued reawakening of Amir's faith, a final reconnection with his heritage.

CONTEXT A04

In a case of life mirroring art, just as Amir becomes involved in a rebuilding project in Afghanistan, so author Khaled Hosseini urged his publisher to donate money for a primary school in northern Afghanistan.

STUDY FOCUS: RECURRING THEMES A02

The re-emergence of the storybook signals a return to the **motif** of stories and storytelling, and also shows Amir trying to find a way to connect with the boy. Following the suicide attempt, Amir feels the need to reconnect with Sohrab, but also to apologise to the boy for letting him down. The book is his way to try to achieve this, and in the process it represents a reconnection with Hassan.

THE END OF THE JOURNEY

There are signs in this chapter that Amir's journey to find himself is at an end. The first is when he looks at the photograph of Hassan and, instead of the turmoil he expects, finds a peace inside himself. He reflects on his old pain 'gathering its things, packing up, and slipping away unannounced in the middle of the night' (p. 313). The next comes when he stands up to his father-in-law's racist attitude to Sohrab, telling him, in formal adult terms, 'You will never again refer to him as "Hazara boy" in my presence' (p. 315). This is a reaction to the kind of comment that Amir has ignored in the past. Taking a stand against it shows a newfound strength and confidence, similar to that of his father.

THE KITE RUNNER

The story returns to its main motif, kite flying, with another scene in which the weather – clouds clearing to produce sunny skies – reflects the emotional tone of the scene. Sohrab has been withdrawn since his suicide attempt and his move to the USA. However, kite flying, an activity which Hassan shared with both Amir and Sohrab, finally brings them closer together. Amir then offers to run the kite for Sohrab, reversing the roles which existed between him and Hassan. As he runs he utters Hassan's phrase 'For you, a thousand times over' (p. 323) and returns to the lyrical prose which he has used to describe the most significant things in his life, showing his loyalty and devotion to the boy.

> **CHECK THE POEM** **A03**
>
> A famous example of **pathetic fallacy** can be found in William Wordsworth's poem, 'I Wandered Lonely as a Cloud' (1807).

GLOSSARY

300	**iodine and peroxide** chemicals used as antiseptics
	gurney trolley used for moving patients in a hospital
305	**ICU** Intensive Care Unit
307	*aush* stew
316	**Hamid Karzai** Afghan president after 2004
319	*Loya jirga* grand assembly
	morgh kabob grilled chicken kebab
320	*seh-parcha* type of fabric
	Sawl-e-nau mubabrak Happy New Year
322	*sabagh* lesson

KEY QUOTATIONS: CHAPTER 25 **A01**

Key quotation 1: Amir tells the story of how he realised that Afghan culture was different and that all any Afghan wanted to know was: 'Was there happiness at the end' (p. 311).

Possible interpretations:

- Amir is a novelist and so the concept of a happy ending is important to him. He is aware, however, that happy endings are not guaranteed in real life.

- This shows Amir's awareness that he may now live in America but will always be an Afghan. He has finally accepted his heritage.

- Hosseini is communicating knowingly with readers who as the conclusion of the book draws closer, want to know if there will be happiness at the end.

Key quotation 2: As Amir sets off to run the kite for Sohrab, he utters Hassan's old phrase: 'For you, a thousand times over.' (p. 323)

Possible interpretations:

- Amir is showing that he no longer thinks of himself as better than his ex-servant.

- As a final act of penance, Amir has swapped places. Sohrab – Hassan's son – is now in Amir's old position, and Amir is Sohrab's servant.

- With one Afghan child saved from the Taliban, the use of the word 'thousand' reminds us that there are many more to be saved.

REVISION FOCUS: TASK 16 **A04** **A02**

How far do you agree with the following statements?

- Amir is an unconventional Afghan.
- *The Kite Runner* is a novel with a 'happy' ending.

Try writing opening paragraphs for essays based on these discussion points. Set out your arguments clearly.

CHARACTERS

AMIR

WHO IS AMIR?

- Amir is the main character and the **narrator** of the story.
- Amir comes from a family who are part of the Pashtun, the ethnic group which has the most power and influence in Afghanistan.
- As an adult, Amir becomes a writer.

THE NARRATOR

The whole story is told by Amir during a period between December 2001 and March 2002 but covers events in Amir's life from his childhood in the early 1970s up to his present. Unlike other characters, we are never given a description of Amir, so our picture of him comes from his voice.

A PEACEFUL BEGINNING

The young Amir lives in an Afghanistan which has been at relative peace for decades and is a stable environment, different from the country of the early twenty-first century. This allows Amir to present himself as a happy and settled child who enjoys his life and his friendship with Hassan, the Hazara boy who is also his servant.

STUDY FOCUS: AN UNRELIABLE NARRATOR A01

In many modern novels, we are presented with a narrator whose own emotional involvement in the story means we cannot always trust what they say. Near the beginning of the novel Amir tells us 'I never thought of Hassan and me as friends' (p. 22), suggesting that he felt distanced from Hassan, probably due to their different ethnicity and statuses in life. However, this is an early sign that we cannot always rely on the things Amir chooses to tell us because it is clear from the tales he relates that Hassan was indeed his closest friend. The desire to distance himself from the boy is a result of his childhood jealousy and also of his later guilt colouring earlier events.

A DEFINING FRIENDSHIP

The major influence in Amir's life is Hassan. Although they are only friends for the first thirteen years of Amir's life, it is clear that this is the defining relationship in his life. This can be inferred from the fact that the novel itself is named after Hassan, but also from the way in which every event that Amir relates ties back to the other boy, either in terms of their great friendship, or in terms of Amir's guilt over his betrayal of that friendship, such as on his wedding day when he wonders if Hassan has married and 'whose face he had seen in the mirror under the veil' (p. 149). Even at such an intimate moment, his thoughts turn to Hassan.

THE SOURCE OF IDENTITY

Amir tells us himself in the opening line of the novel that the person he is now was formed on the day in the alley in 1975. Although we don't find out for another five chapters what this event was, everything we are told, both before and after the revelation, is tinged with the emotions of anger, guilt and sorrow emerging from it.

However, as well as being a burden, his feelings about Hassan are also a positive force in Amir's life. His desire to write grows from by his time spent reading stories to Hassan. His later success as a writer can be seen to emerge from a desire to assuage his guilt by doing something which he knows Hassan would enjoy and approve of, thanks to the stories they shared as children. Also, his marriage to Soraya and his yearning for children can be seen as his way of recreating the situation of his own childhood but this time with the chance to make up for his past mistakes. This idea is even more powerfully emphasised when the story moves to modern-day Kabul at the end of the novel. When Rahim Khan asks Amir to save Sohrab, Amir is really being given a second chance to save his friend.

SEARCHING FOR LOVE

One blot on Amir's early life is the lack of love and respect which he feels he gets from his father. The first half of the novel concerns the tensions which Amir feels in his life between wanting to be his own man and the desire to be the man his father wants him to be. This is also a central factor, so he tells us, in his decision not to help Hassan during the attack in the alley.

A LONG SHADOW

Although Baba no longer features as a character in the events being related after his death, he is still a presence in Amir's life, and Amir's decision to revisit Kabul and to retrieve Sohrab can be seen as his attempt to finally reconcile his feelings for his father. By standing up to Assef and literally fighting for possession of Sohrab, who is Baba's grandson, Amir finds a way to become the man his father wanted him to be. This is demonstrated further upon his return to the USA when he becomes involved in building a hospital in Afghanistan just as his father had built the orphanage.

THE STORYTELLER

Another main strand of Amir's life, and one which runs contrary to his father's wishes, is his interest in stories and writing. This is an inherited trait from his mother who was a teacher of literature. It also provides an escape, first from the perceived lack of love from his father, and later from having to acknowledge the problems in his life and in his homeland. Writing is seen as a retreat and it is telling that, upon his return to Afghanistan, he admits that he is not currently writing about the country. Instead he has written most recently about 'a university professor who joins a clan of gypsies after he finds his wife in bed with one of his students' (p. 206). Thinking about this book in the context of his current location he continues, 'But suddenly I was embarrassed by it. I hoped Wahid wouldn't ask what it was about' (p. 206).

The Kite Runner can be seen as Amir's attempt to write a book about Afghanistan, and in doing so to place himself back in context. Amir makes his life into a **narrative** in an attempt to make sense of his actions and to understand his anxieties. This arrangement of the events of his life into a coherent story can be seen as an act of **catharsis**.

> **CONTEXT** **A04**
>
> 'The setting in 1970s Kabul, the house where Amir lived, the films that he watches, of course the kite flying, the love of storytelling – all of that is from my own childhood. The story line is fictional' (Khaled Hosseini, interview with Erika Milvy on www.salon.com).

REVISION FOCUS: TASK 17 **A02**

How far do you agree with the following statements?

● Amir's search for redemption is also a search for the lost love of his mother.

● Amir could not truly become a man while Baba was still alive.

Try writing opening paragraphs for essays based on these discussion points. Set out your arguments clearly.

HASSAN

WHO IS HASSAN?

- Hassan is the 'kite runner' of the book's title.
- He is Amir's childhood friend and protector, and is later revealed to be his half-brother.
- He is a Hazara, a member of an ethnic group discriminated against in Afghanistan.

THE KITE RUNNER

As the 'kite runner' of the title, Hassan is arguably the most significant character in the novel. While Amir is the **narrator**, and the novel is the relating of his story, Hassan's story and what he represents to Amir, and to Baba, are the crucial driving forces in the novel. This is all the more remarkable given that he disappears from Amir's story relatively early on, and reappears only in Rahim Khan's story and one posthumous letter. He exists in most of the novel as a presence, looming over the **narrative**, rather than as a character taking parts in events.

A HAPPY BOY

We are presented with a very clear physical description of Hassan in Chapter 2, including his 'flat, broad nose and slanting, narrow eyes like bamboo leaves' (p. 3), his 'tiny low-set ears and … pointed stub of a chin' (p. 3) and the cleft lip which is corrected in Chapter 5. However, as mentioned above, all that we learn about Hassan, apart from the one letter with which we are presented in Chapter 17, comes via Amir's perception of him. What we are told is therefore one person's perspective on Hassan. The portrait which Amir paints is of a boy much more at ease with himself and his place in the world than Amir himself, and than we might expect from his situation. Hassan is a servant but does not seem to resent this. He is also burdened with an ill father and the fact that, as a Hazara, he lives in a country which looks down on his ethnic group. However, he receives a great deal of warmth and love from Ali and so does not suffer from the same need to strive for his father's affections which is so much a feature of Amir's life.

READ BETWEEN THE LINES

Up to the point of the rape, the hardships with which Hassan has to live do not seem to bother him very much. This may be a true picture of the young servant, but we must remember that the tales of Hassan are coloured by thirty years of Amir's guilt. As a consequence of this guilt, Amir feels the need to remember his friend as happy and carefree up to the point of his betrayal. In order to get a true impression of Hassan we must be aware of Amir's self-editing and look to the letter that Hassan writes to Amir twenty-five years after they last see each other.

GROWING UP FAST

As we follow Hassan's story, it is clear that he has been forced to grow up faster than Amir. Although Hassan is a year younger than Amir, at times he acts more like an adult. In Chapter 6, he is happy to let Amir win at cards, knowing that to do otherwise might provoke an outburst. During this game, Amir offers, when they have grown up, to buy him a television to which Hassan replies, 'I'll put it on my table, where I keep my drawings' (p. 51). This comment makes Amir sad because it shows that Hassan believes his life will never change or improve, and that he will always live in the same hut he currently shares with his father.

AN ADULT CHILD

Another of Hassan's significant characteristics is the resignation with which he greets both Amir's question about eating dirt and the incident where Amir hits him with the pomegranate. The willingness to take whatever is forced upon him shows a child who is used to carrying burdens and coming off second best; who is willing to take responsibility for Amir's actions without comment. This comparison can be extended by considering the way that Hassan responds to Amir's enquiry about eating dirt in simple, non-judgemental tones – 'Would you ever ask me to do such a thing, Amir agha?' (p. 48) – and later, during the pomegranate incident, by literally turning his cheek.

STUDY FOCUS: LETTERS · A02

Letters are often used in literature to allow characters other than the narrator to speak directly to the reader. The only time we are presented with Hassan's direct voice, rather than it being filtered through Amir's perceptions, is in the letter he gives to Rahim Khan to pass to Amir. The letter is written by an adult Hassan, not the child of Amir's recollections, but it throws light on the character of Hassan as he must have been, even as a child. He opens and closes the letter with religious invocations. While Amir has mentioned Hassan's beliefs, they are obviously of greater importance to Hassan than we might assume from Amir's tales. The letter continues with a kind and considerate tone, using phrases such as 'I pray that this letter finds you in good health' (p. 189). It is clear that Hassan does not hold a grudge against Amir for his past actions and is not weighed down by those actions as Amir is. Hassan signs off his letter by referring to himself as Amir's friend, something which Amir could never bring himself to do. It shows us that Hassan's love and loyalty to his former master have not waned over the years.

CHECK THE BOOK · A03

The technique of using letters and a range of **first-person narrators** has been used to construct whole novels. One famous example is Bram Stoker's *Dracula* (1897).

KEY QUOTATION: HASSAN · A01

Key quotation: The phrase which sums up Hassan for Amir is related to us very early on in the novel: '*For you, a thousand times over*' (p. 1).

Possible interpretations:

- This phrase is one of utter loyalty, showing Hassan's devotion to Amir.
- The fact that Amir remembers this so often shows that it is a source of guilt for him that he took Hassan's loyalty for granted.
- The phrase displays a pure emotion. Its plain-spoken honesty contrasts with Amir's secrets and lies.

BABA

WHO IS BABA?

- Baba is Amir and Hassan's father.
- He is an important and influential businessman in Kabul.
- Even in America, Baba's personality is enough to make him a respected and well-liked man.

AN IMPRESSIVE FIGURE

Once again what we learn about Baba is mostly from Amir's perspective. Amir is very proud of his father and somewhat in awe of him. Therefore Baba is often painted as a larger-than-life character who is almost unbelievably charismatic and successful. Amir describes him as 'a towering Pashtun specimen with a thick beard, a wayward crop of curly brown hair' and 'hands that looked capable of uprooting a willow tree' (p. 11). Given the way Amir sees his father it would be easy to assume that this is an overstatement. However, as corroboration, Amir adds a quotation from Rahim Khan that Baba had a 'black glare that would "drop the devil to his knees begging for mercy"' (p. 11).

STUDY FOCUS: SHOW, DON'T TELL — A02

Readers are rarely told what to think of characters in books. Instead the author presents them to the readers who are then allowed to make up their own minds. By interpreting what Amir says about his father and looking at the ways in which other people are reported to act around him we can put together an understanding of his character. From the reactions of the man who kisses Baba's hand after Baba prevents the Russian soldier from raping his wife, and the men in the bar in Hayward who become friends and admirers of Baba in a single evening after Amir's graduation, it is clear that, unless Amir's account of his father is entirely fictitious, Baba has a powerfully charismatic personality which affects the people around him.

POWERFUL AND GENEROUS

Baba is a successful man. He lives in a large house, which he built himself, in a wealthy and respectable part of Kabul. We know this last fact not merely from Amir's reports but from the fact that under the rule of the Taliban the elite of Afghanistan's regime choose to live in that area, and in that house in particular. In addition, the building of an orphanage is the act of a wealthy man. It is also, however, the act of a concerned member of society, a benefactor and a man with a love of children. This is not a side of Baba that Amir reveals so often – in large part due to his own feelings of alienation from his father's love.

A MAN OR A MYTH?

The story that Amir tells of his father wrestling with a black bear gives us an example of the high regard in which Amir holds his father. It sounds more like a myth or a fable than a true anecdote and suggests that Amir's regard is almost a form of worship of his father as some kind of god or idol. Indeed, Amir tells us that he dreams about his father wrestling with the bear, and that 'in those dreams, I can never tell Baba from the bear' (p. 11).

CONTEXT — A04

Although we are not given another name for him, Baba is actually the Arabic word for 'father'.

CONTEXT — A04

We are told that Baba was born in 1933, the same year in which Zahir Shah started his forty-year peaceful reign of Afghanistan. It was also the year in which Adolf Hitler was appointed Chancellor of Germany.

CHECK THE BOOK — A03

Oil (1927), by Upton Sinclair, which was made into the 2007 film *There Will Be Blood*, also concerns a son who struggles to live up to his father's expectations.

LONELINESS

One key to Baba's character is the loss of his wife, Sofia, at the moment of Amir's birth. Amir believes that Baba hates him for causing Sofia's death. While this is probably untrue and is, in fact, another product of Amir's guilt and poor self-esteem, it is certain that this loss affected his father. Baba does not remarry, nor are we told of any other women in his life, other than his affair with Sanaubar, so we can assume that he still thinks of Sofia as his wife and does not want to replace her. With regard to the influence of this on his relationship with Amir, it is doubtful that he blames his son for her death, but it is likely that Amir reminds Baba of Sofia with the love of books and reading that comes from his mother. This would account, to some extent, for the distance that Amir feels between him and his father. Baba can allow himself to feel closer to his other son, Hassan, because there is not the same set of associations.

DRIVEN BY GUILT

A second key to Baba's character comes from the revelation that he is Hassan's father. This sheds light on his actions all the way through the novel. Part of Amir's alienation from his father stems from the way that he insists on treating Hassan equally to him. Only when Amir realises that Hassan was actually his half-brother can he come to see this treatment as fair, rather than an insult whereby he is seen to be of no more importance to his father than the servant's son.

Baba's need to overcome his guilt over his affair with Sanaubar, and his torment at his inability to publicly name Hassan as his son, in many ways make him the driven and proud man who is presented to us through Amir's **narrative**.

KEY QUOTATION: BABA A01

Key quotation: Amir introduces his father with the phrase: 'Lore has it my father once wrestled a black bear in Baluchistan with his bare hands' (p. 11).

Possible interpretations:

- If true, this would make Baba a very strong and impressive man. True or not, it is the first memory that Amir shares with us, showing his high opinion of his father.
- There is an indication that Amir doubts this story as he qualifies it by saying that 'Lore has it …'.
- By 'lore' Amir means that this is what he has heard from other people. It shows the regard for Baba which the community holds. This regard is more important than whether or not the story is true.

CONTEXT A03

Fights with bears and beasts are a common way of showing bravery (or cowardice) in literature. Compare Baba to Antigonus in Shakespeare's, *The Winter's Tale*, who famously exits the stage 'pursued by a bear' (iii.3.57), and is then killed by it.

ALI

WHO IS ALI?

- Ali is the servant in Baba's household. He was Baba's childhood friend and raised Hassan as his son.

THE SERVANT

Ali is presented as Hassan's father and a childhood friend of Baba. His relationship with Amir's father is a direct reflection of Hassan's relationship with Amir. Left as an orphan at a young age, Ali was brought up by Baba's father's servants and was a servant to Baba in the same way that Hassan was brought up as a servant to Amir.

A TARGET

Having suffered from polio as a child Ali has one withered leg and walks with a profound limp. This makes him an object of fun for the neighbourhood children who are happy to tease and bully him. In the same way as Hassan he also carries the stigma of being a Hazara. We are told that 'Of all the neighborhood boys who tortured Ali, Assef was by far the most relentless' (p. 34). It is, to some extent, the fact of who his father is that leads to Hassan being a target of Assef and his friends.

STRONG AND LOYAL

Although we later find out that Hassan is not his son, Ali does not seem upset by this and treats Hassan with all the love and respect that we can imagine he would have given his biological son. This shows a man who is kind and compassionate as well as loyal. This last aspect is emphasised when Ali and Hassan have to leave Baba's house. Ali obviously knows what Amir has done, and also what he has failed to do, but does not reveal these things to Baba. Hassan has sworn him to secrecy and, even though revealing all to Baba would allow them to stay, and would give Ali a way to get back at Baba for his affair with Sanaubar, Ali keeps his promise to Hassan, and says nothing. This shows that Ali, although mostly in the background of the story, is a man of strong character, and much more of an equal to Baba than Amir is to Hassan.

REVISION FOCUS: TASK 18 · A02

How far do you agree with the following statement?

- Hassan is more Ali's son than Baba's.

Try writing an opening paragraph for an essay based on this discussion point. Set out your arguments clearly.

RAHIM KHAN

WHO IS RAHIM KHAN?

- Rahim Khan is Baba's best friend and business colleague. He is also a surrogate father to Amir.

CONTEXT · A04

Ali's name is **symbolic** of his ethnicity as a Hazara and his religious leanings as a Shi'a rather than a Sunni Muslim. The Shi'as believe that Ali (the cousin and son-in-law of Muhammad) was the true inheritor of the Islamic faith.

ANOTHER FATHER

Rahim Khan is Baba's friend and business colleague. He is a constant presence in Amir's childhood. Where Baba is portrayed as powerful and sometimes dismissive of Amir, Rahim Khan is shown to be sensitive and patient, and provides a balance for Baba. He acts as a surrogate parent for Amir, providing the support, guidance and understanding that he fails to get from his father, and can't get from his mother because of her absence. Rahim Khan is a positive influence on Amir and provides him with the foundations for his later success.

CONTEXT **A04**

The name Rahim means 'compassionate', a title which elegantly sums up the role Rahim Khan plays in Amir's life.

STUDY FOCUS: A GUIDE **A02**

The 'guide' or 'mentor' is a common type of character in novels that feature a young **protagonist** growing into maturity – like Amir. This character is often an older man who can provide advice to the protagonist, but also force them into action when the need arises. Rahim Khan is such a character. He reappears later in the novel, but this time as a figure of redemption. Having been such a strong presence in Amir's childhood, he is one of the few people who could cause him to come back to Afghanistan and force him to face his childhood fears and mistakes. Having guided Amir through his childhood, he now acts as his mentor as he moves into adulthood and maturity.

REVISION FOCUS: TASK 19 **A02**

How far do you agree with the following statement?

● When Rahim Khan calls Amir back to Pakistan he is seeking atonement for his own silence over the attack on Hassan.

Try writing an opening paragraph for an essay based on this discussion point. Set out your arguments clearly.

SORAYA

WHO IS SORAYA?

● Soraya is Amir's wife and the daughter of an Afghan general.

LYRICAL LOVE

When we first meet Soraya, Amir describes her in a series of vivid images which reflect his feelings for her. From his first impressions of 'the way her luminous eyes had fleetingly held mine' (p. 124), to their wedding when 'A blush, red like henna, bloomed on her cheeks' (p. 149) to his return to the USA, when he 'smelled apples in her hair' (p. 312), Amir reserves his most colourful and poetic **imagery** for his descriptions of his wife.

A REFLECTION OF GUILT

Soraya is similar to Amir's mother in that she is a teacher but, like Amir, she has her own guilty past which lays a burden on her (see Chapter 12). Unlike Amir she is able to give up her burden and move on with her life. In this way she acts as a reflection of Amir's inability to do these things.

CHILDLESS

The implication in the text is that the infertility that Soraya and Amir suffer from is Soraya's rather than Amir's, especially as Amir tells us that he passed his fertility test 'with flying colors' (p. 161). However, it would seem, in **metaphorical** terms, that the infertility results from Amir's failure to fully grow up and to move away from his childhood. It is only

CHECK THE BOOK **A03**

In *Pride and Prejudice* (1813) by Jane Austen, sixteen-year-old Lydia Bennet runs away with a soldier, Mr Wickham. In order to save the family honour, Wickham is paid to marry her.

at the end of the story that he appears to earn the gift of a child. This part of the story reflects the history of Ali, Baba and Hassan. Just as Ali was unable to father a child and was given Hassan by Baba, so Amir and Soraya are given Sohrab courtesy of Hassan.

INVOKING THE PAST

Soraya was the name of the wife of King Amanullah Khan, the reforming king of Afghanistan who was the first ruler of the country following the final Anglo-Afghan war. By using her name, Hosseini connects the story back to a more hopeful and peaceful time in Afghanistan's history.

CONTEXT A04

The name Soraya means 'princess' just as the name Amir means 'prince'.

ASSEF

WHO IS ASSEF?

- Assef is Amir's childhood bully and, later, a high-ranking member of the Taliban in Afghanistan.

THE BULLY

Assef is both a bully and later a member of the Taliban. This indicates that the treatment of the Afghan people by the Taliban is a form of bullying, but on a larger and more comprehensively violent scale. However, the fact that Assef wears Western-style sunglasses and has a sexual preference for children indicates that he does not hold to the strict moral and religious code that the Taliban espouse and that he is simply using them as a cover to follow his own twisted agenda.

CHECK THE BOOK A03

A sociopath is someone who does not have any concern for the normal moral rules of society or the effects their actions have on others, such as Hannibal Lecter in Thomas Harris's *The Silence of the Lambs* (1988).

STUDY FOCUS: THE BAD GUY A02

For every **protagonist** there needs to be an antagonist – a bad guy – for them to overcome. Assef fills this role. However, he also provides a larger understanding of the issues in the novel. Amir describes Assef as a 'sociopath'. This means he has no regard for the rights or feelings of others or for laws, and is happy to violate those rights and laws without regard to the consequences. By placing Assef at the centre of the most violent and disturbing parts of the novel – bullying, rape, mass murder, execution, etc. – we see how the problems in Afghanistan over the time period covered by the novel are also a result of the pervasive violation of rights and laws by and against many different groups. One group which is particularly victimised is the Hazaras, and Assef's relationships with both Ali and Hassan are representative of this.

EXTREMISM

Assef's professed love of Hitler is also a significant element of his character. This tells us immediately about his extreme views and instability and provides a short-hand way of understanding his intentions and beliefs.

SOHRAB

WHO IS SOHRAB?

- Sohrab is Hassan's son. After Hassan's death he is rescued from Kabul and eventually adopted by Amir.

AMIR'S REDEMPTION

Sohrab is, at least in Amir's eyes, a substitute for Hassan. By saving the boy from the orphanage he is finally able to make up for not saving Hassan from the rape in the alley. Sohrab does not, however, have the same resigned attitude as his father and, when pressed, takes a stand against further brutality by attempting suicide. This in large part can be seen as the result of the more traumatic upbringing he has had, with constant violence in Kabul, the death of his parents and his abuse at the hands of the Taliban.

STUDY FOCUS: ABANDONED   A01

Sohrab continues a dynasty of discarded children, starting with Ali who was made an orphan at an early age, moving down through Hassan who was both illegitimate and abandoned by his mother, and finally to Sohrab who is also orphaned. These three characters are representative of their ethnic group, the Hazara, who could be said to be orphaned and abandoned by the Afghan state. If this **metaphor** is continued, however, then the rescue of Sohrab by Amir, an ethnic Pashtun, suggests a potentially positive future for the remaining Hazaras, with a reconciliation and drawing back into the mainstream.

SOFIA AND SANAUBAR

WHO ARE SOFIA AND SANAUBAR?

- Sofia is Amir's mother and Baba's wife. She dies giving birth to Amir.
- Sanaubar is Hassan's mother. She leaves Ali after Hassan's birth but returns many years later, shortly before her death.

ABSENT MOTHERS

Sofia and Sanaubar are the absent mothers of Amir and Hassan. Sofia, a teacher at the university, died while giving birth to Amir. She is therefore absent in his life but present through his love of books, reading and writing. Because of her untimely death she becomes a **symbol** for both Amir and Baba of things that are good and pure. When Amir later meets a beggar in the devastated Kabul who knew his mother, this is a sign that a memory of goodness can prevail even through the hardest of times.

GUILT IN DEATH

Amir also carries guilt over the death of his mother, believing that the distance he feels between himself and his father is due to Baba blaming him for her death. It is not stated in the novel, but it would seem reasonable that when he finds out that the cause of this distance between them is, in fact, Baba's secret fathering of Hassan, Amir would be able to dispense with this aspect of his guilt.

DISHONOUR AND FORGIVENESS

Sanaubar, in contrast to Sofia, is depicted in earthy terms as a sexy and sexually active woman who Amir describes as a 'beautiful but notoriously unscrupulous woman who lived up to her dishonourable reputation' (p. 7). Unlike Sofia, she did not die, but instead deserted Hassan shortly after his birth. Again, this in part can be explained by her unfaithfulness to Ali with Baba. Many years later she returns and we see from Hassan's reaction that he has felt great resentment at her betrayal. However, true to his character, he forgives her and she is welcomed back into the family, becoming a beloved grandmother to Sohrab.

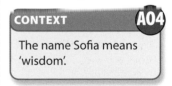

CONTEXT   A04

The name Sofia means 'wisdom'.

THEMES

FATHERS AND SONS

CHECK THE BOOK A03

The relationship between fathers and sons is a common one in literature and a popular topic in Shakespeare's plays, most notably in *Hamlet*, where Hamlet discovers that his uncle has killed his father.

BABA AND AMIR

The Kite Runner examines the relationships between men in the absence of women, and in particular the relationships between fathers and their sons. The most prominent relationship is the problematic one between Baba and Amir. Baba has mixed feelings about Amir, both because of Sofia's death and because he is the father of Hassan. While Amir is unaware of the second of these reasons he feels that his father is not as warm to him as he would like. His attempts to close the distance between them have a great influence on his personality and the events of his life.

The relationship is finally reconciled on Baba's part when he sees his son grow into a man and get married. This is made clear when Amir discovers that Soraya has been reading his stories to his father. Baba says, 'I put her up to it. I hope you don't mind' (p. 151). Not only is he admitting to the fact that he wanted to hear the stories that he had previously dismissed, but he seeks his son's forgiveness, an act of respect that we have not seen previously.

HASSAN

Baba never acknowledges the fact that he is Hassan's father and therefore always carries the guilt for this and his betrayal of Ali. Hassan has a positive relationship with Baba who treats him as Amir's equal. Hassan does not have to cope with any of the animosity or guilt he might feel if he knew his true parentage. Ali meanwhile, fulfils the role of father for Hassan. He, too, carries the secret of Hassan's parentage, but as he is able to pretend that Hassan is actually his son, it does not seem to affect him in the same way as it does Baba. From Amir's descriptions, it seems that Ali has a closer relationship with Hassan than Baba has with and Amir.

SOHRAB

Another pairing of father and son comes in the form of Hassan and Sohrab. Their lives and relationship mirror those of Ali and Hassan, but with the added fact that Hassan is Sohrab's natural father. As the novel comes to a close, Amir has replaced Hassan as Sohrab's guardian, which provides a reflection of Ali raising Baba's son as Amir now raises Hassan's, suggesting that the acts of caring, loving and guiding are as influential as blood ties.

RAHIM KHAN

Rahim Khan is also a father figure: he acts as a surrogate father to Amir. When the relationship between Amir and Baba is strained, Rahim Khan provides support and comfort. In his later role, providing Amir with a chance to make amends, he does and says things that Baba may have wished to do and say, and finds a way for Amir to reconcile both himself and Hassan with their father. In his letter he tells Amir, 'I want you to understand that good, *real* good, was born out of your father's remorse' (p. 263). Through this we understand that the actions which had made Baba such a legend in Amir's eyes were driven in large part by his remorse over Hassan's parentage. This allows Amir to equate his own guilt with his father's and therefore feel closer to him.

REDEMPTION

'A WAY TO BE GOOD AGAIN'

A major theme in the novel is the search for redemption. Amir's story is encapsulated in the offer made to him by Rahim Khan in the opening chapter, *'There is a way to be good again'* (p. 2). It is the desire to make up for the events of his childhood, and the fear of what it might cost him to achieve this, which drive all of Amir's decisions in the novel and form the basis for his character.

THE NEED TO RETURN

Amir's return to Afghanistan is a key part of this search for redemption, because by going to the USA – and fitting in so well there – he has effectively run away from the events of his childhood, and also from his heritage and all the things which should form the person he is. Only by returning can he match up the person he is with the person he wants to be. He returns and rescues Sohrab from the Taliban and, in doing so, **symbolically** rescues Hassan from the bullies, thus finally making up for his lack of action all those years ago.

BABA'S GUILT

Amir is not the only character searching for redemption. His father, both in public activities such as building an orphanage and in the private ways in which he interacts with his two sons, is searching for a way to atone for his infidelity with Sanaubar and his inability to acknowledge Hassan. He also feels a need to improve his relationship with Amir, which has been damaged by his guilt. While he never gets a chance to resolve his remorse over Ali and Hassan, he and Amir become much closer during their time in the USA.

PARTNERS IN REDEMPTION

Soraya is also seeking redemption for past sins. This is one reason why she and Amir would seem to be such a good match. He is in a position to understand her need for forgiveness and is therefore able, when she informs him of her disgrace, to reply 'Nothing you said changes anything. I want us to marry' (p. 144). Later, when he finds out more details, he once more dismisses the topic, adding 'Let's never talk about this again' (p. 157).

VICARIOUS REDEMPTION

Rahim Khan is also seeking redemption. He carries guilt over his failure to speak up at a time when it could have made a difference, regarding both Hassan's rape and his parentage. Unable to seek atonement for himself, his request that Amir rescues Sohrab from Kabul is his way of achieving this redemption.

KEY QUOTATION: REDEMPTION `A01`

Key quotation: When Hassan and Ali leave Baba's house, Amir imagines, 'I'd chase the car … I'd pull Hassan out of the backseat and tell him I was sorry, so sorry' (p. 94).

Possible interpretations:

- Amir is a storyteller, so it is easier for him to imagine this than it is for him to actually do it.
- Looking back, this is a key moment for the adult Amir, as it was his last chance to make things right.
- This is a poignant moment, as Amir never sees Hassan again and never gets to actually say the words he most wants to say: 'I'm sorry'.

CHECK THE POEM `A03`

'Redemption', a religious poem by Frederick William Orde Ward (published 1916), promises that however much pain is suffered in life, the power of redemption will heal it.

RELIGION AND ETHNICITY

ALWAYS AN AFGHAN

Amir, like his father, is not a devout Muslim. The only times he reverts to prayer are during moments of fear and distress. However, his nominal religion and his ethnicity form key parts of the **narrative** for him and for all the other characters.

Although Amir's is mostly a journey of redemption, this is tied in with the idea of what it means to be an Afghan. Part of the problem in Amir's relationship with his father results from Baba's idea of what an Afghan man should be like. Baba's image of himself as an Afghan informs both his bravery in the face of the Russian soldier, and also his anger and confusion when asked for identification in the American mini-market. His ethnicity is an integral part of him and so, when Amir does not match up to his image of what it means to be an Afghan man, this drives them further apart.

THE IMMIGRANT EXPERIENCE

The suggestion that Amir does not fit in as an Afghan is reinforced by the ease with which he slots into American society. This is demonstrated by his descriptions of his studies in the USA, his house and his success as a writer. It is also clear from how he feels upon his return to Afghanistan. Amir tells Farid that he feels like a tourist in his own country, and Farid replies that Amir has always been a tourist. The attainment of Farid's respect coincides with Amir finally feeling more comfortable in his home country.

ETHNIC TENSION

The tensions between the Pashtuns and Hazaras form a thread throughout the novel. The teasing and bullying of Ali and Hassan occur because of their ethnicity, and the befriending by Baba and Amir of these Hazaras is across this ethnic divide. Baba seems to be more advanced in his opinions than many of his fellow Afghans, and passes this liberal attitude onto his son. However, Amir does not act on these beliefs until the end of the novel when he tells his father-in-law to refer to Sohrab by name rather than by his ethnic group.

Farid demonstrates the same discriminatory views as were present in Amir's childhood, showing that this is still a problem in Afghanistan. Hosseini seems to be suggesting that the lack of respect for different peoples underlies the problems in Afghanistan.

SPIRITUALITY

Hassan, Ali and Sohrab, as Hazaras, are shown as being much more spiritual and devout than Amir and his father. Amir refers to Hassan having 'prayed the morning *namaz* with Ali' (p. 23) while he is still emerging from his bed, having taken no part in the morning prayers. However, this devotion does not save them from the Taliban because the Taliban follow the Sunni branch of Islam, while Ali and Hassan are Shi'a muslims. As Hazaras and Shi'a muslims, Hassan and his family face both religious and ethnic persecution.

CONTEXT **A04**

Pashtun and Hazara are just two of the ethnic groups which make up Afghanistan's diverse racial mix. Other groups include Tajiks, Uzbeks and nomadic Aimak.

CONTEXT **A04**

Hazarajat, a region in the centre of Afghanistan, is the native homeland of the Hazara people. It has been a part of Afghanistan since the late nineteenth century, but was previously under the rule of many races, including Greeks, Persians, Turks and Mongols.

KEY QUOTATION: RELIGION AND ETHNICITY   **A01**

Key quotation: In Islamabad, Sohrab runs away. The hotel manager tells Amir: 'The thing about you Afghanis is that … well, you people are a little reckless' (p. 275).

Possible interpretations:

● This shows the opinion of Afghans held by the Pakistanis which, if true, could account for some of the upheaval in Afghanistan.

● This comment makes Amir laugh as his life has been one of avoiding being reckless.

● This is now a true observation about Amir, as in reconciling himself with his heritage, he has found his bravery and his ability to be reckless.

STORYTELLING

'TELL ME A STORY'

The whole **narrative** of the novel is told to us as a story, with Amir setting the scene for us at the beginning and providing background, and then narrating the story from its end point. As a **narrator** he constantly intrudes into the story, **foreshadowing** events to come, and reminding us that we are being told a story.

The **symbolism** of storytelling is reinforced when Amir tells us of the stories he read to Hassan as a child and about his development into a novelist. The artificial nature of what we are told is regularly foregrounded which forces the reader to interpret the story for its underlying meanings, rather than simply accept it at face value.

TOO PERSONAL

When Wahid tells Amir to write about Afghanistan, Amir says he is not that sort of writer. Hosseini, who is from a similar background to Amir, is of course writing about Afghanistan, which begs the question why Amir is not. This concept is associated with Amir's difficulty in accepting his Afghan heritage, but also places him as a fiction writer who makes things up, rather than describing the real world. The story he is narrating to us therefore demonstrates a change brought about by his return to Afghanistan. *The Kite Runner* is a story that Amir has found too hard to relate previously due to the harsh reality of his homeland and the pain involved in exploring the internal landscape.

STORIES AS SYMBOLS

The stories which are told in the novel all have symbolic value because they are stories of friendship and loyalty. The stories that Amir reads to Hassan form a large part of their bond, but are also used to tease and bully Hassan. Later, however, they provide Hassan with a name for his son – a reference to Amir and Hassan's connection and a gesture of forgiveness from Hassan to Amir. The ultimate reconciliation of Amir and his father comes when Amir discovers that Soraya has been reading his stories to Baba. This act of acceptance finally enables Amir to see his father's love for him.

In the novel, stories also relate to teaching and learning, whether it is Amir's mother's book being the source of her teaching materials, Amir failing to teach Hassan to read or Soraya teaching her servant to read. So, when Amir has finally learned his lesson he buys a copy of the book that he used to share with Hassan. Rather than using it to mislead and tease, he now plans to use it to build a bridge to Sohrab.

ANOTHER POINT OF VIEW

The letters from Hassan and Rahim Khan and Rahim Khan's tale of his time in Kabul after Amir and his father left give us an alternative perspective from Amir's story. This distance allows us to judge how truthful Amir's narrative has been.

KEY QUOTATION: STORYTELLING   A01

Key quotation: Amir reads stories to Hassan who is held spell-bound by them. Amir tells us that 'Words were secret doorways and I held all the keys' (p. 26).

Possible interpretations:

- This is the first time we see what Amir will become – a writer – and it is fitting that it is Hassan's love for the stories he hears that spurs Amir on.
- The use of the word 'secret' is important here, because soon after he has read these stories Amir will have a secret for which he does have the words and keys.
- Amir's faith in words to unlock the world is perhaps what prevents him from taking action.

CHECK THE BOOK   A03

Storytelling is a key theme in Persian literature as exemplified by the classic text *One Thousand and One Nights* (sometimes called *The Arabian Nights*) which includes 'Aladdin and His Magic Lamp', 'Ali Baba and the Forty Thieves' and 'The Seven Voyages of Sinbad'.

CONTEXT   A04

The term for a piece of fiction that addresses the act of storytelling as one of its themes is 'metafiction'. It literally means 'fiction about fiction'. By featuring a novelist as the **protagonist**, relating the story to us as a potentially fictionalised account of the real story, *The Kite Runner* could be viewed as a metafiction.

HISTORY

HIS STORY

While *The Kite Runner* is the story of Amir, Hassan and their father, it is also a story about the events in Afghanistan from the 1970s to the first years of the twenty-first century. Hosseini uses the story of Amir to tell the story of Afghanistan at the same time, intertwining the two so that the history does not become either a backdrop or an interruption, but an integral part of the plot and **narrative**.

A REAL-LIFE BACKGROUND

There are many examples of real events occurring in the novel, starting with the sounds of the coup in 1973 intruding on Amir's childhood as the first signs of what is to come. Elsewhere, the experiences of real Afghans are echoed in the events in the novel, such as the flight of Amir and Baba from Khabul, Baba's confrontation with the Russian soldier, the Taliban killing Hassan, and Assef becoming a leader in the Taliban.

Perhaps the greatest **symbolic** interaction of the story and historical events is the banning by the Taliban of kite flying and fighting. By making this sport the centre of the novel, Hosseini is able to show to what extent the Taliban were opposed to the desires and wishes of ordinary Afghan people. For more on the real events that underlie the story, and are bound up in it, see **Part Five: Historical background**.

KEY QUOTATIONS: HISTORY   A01

Key quotation 1: On the verge of responding to Hassan's criticism of his first story, Amir is interrupted by a loud noise. He says 'I never got to finish that sentence. Because suddenly Afghanistan changed forever.' (p. 30)

Possible interpretations:

- The interruption is the sound of a coup taking place on the streets of Kabul. In this we see the large-scale events of history imposing on the small-scale events of Amir's life.

- The change in Afghanistan is also reflected in the change for Amir. His previous life has ceased to exist and the more troubled Afghanistan will be the place of his future.

- Amir's greatest regrets are the things he has left unsaid. Sometimes he doesn't speak as a result of his own decisions, sometimes as a result of historical events that are out of his control.

Key quotation 2: In relating events from his time in America, Amir tells us that 'six months before the Soviets withdrew from Afghanistan, I finished my first novel' (p. 159).

Possible interpretations:

- Despite living in America, Amir's personal timescale is still tied up with events in Afghanistan.

- The moment of liberation for his country comes at the same moment as Amir completes this long-awaited project.

- With hindsight we know that the withdrawal of the Soviets did not lead to a peaceful and happy Afghanistan. Likewise, despite his love of writing, Amir cannot be happy without resolving his other conflicts.

CHECK THE BOOK   A03

The interweaving of fact and fiction is also a feature of the books in Pat Barker's *Regeneration* trilogy: *Regeneration*, *The Eye in the Door* and *The Ghost Road*. These address the events of the First World War and include the real-life war poet Siegfried Sassoon as a character.

CHECK THE POEM   A03

Amir finds it hard to confront Afghanistan's problems in his writing. This predicament is similar to that expressed in Hayden Carruth's poem 'On Being Asked to Write a Poem Against the War in Vietnam' (1992), which examines the futility of being a poet when faced with the topic of war.

PART FOUR: STRUCTURE, FORM AND LANGUAGE

STRUCTURE

LOOKING BACK

The story is told from its chronological end point, so that Amir frequently **foreshadows** events that are yet to come. Using this technique a storyteller undercuts current events by revealing they will not last, as at the end of Chapter 5, 'that was the winter that Hassan stopped smiling' (p. 41). The technique is also used to build tension by revealing a small piece of information about events to come, making the reader want to read on and find out what happens next, as at the end of Chapters 1 and 2, and in particular at the end of Chapter 4, 'I never got to finish that sentence. Because suddenly Afghanistan changed forever' (p. 30).

A CENTRAL MOMENT

This technique of hinting at future events continues to be used after we learn about Hassan's rape, but not as frequently as before, and not usually as a chapter ending. Instead, memories of earlier times are inserted into later chapters, so that the moment of the rape forms the central moment to which earlier chapters look forward and later chapters look back.

STUDY FOCUS: FRACTURE   A02

It is at the moment of Hassan's rape that both the structure and style of the writing change. In terms of the structure, apart from the fragment of Chapter 1, the chapters leading up to the revelation of the attack in the alley are all told in a straightforward manner, although much of what we are told fills in details from the characters' lives prior to the kite fight. Stories unfold in a chronological manner leading up to the event. However, at the moment of the attack the **narrative** structure fractures and never fully resumes the linear structure of earlier chapters. As Amir witnesses the rape the narrative veers to other stories at other times, representing Amir's subconscious need to avoid dealing with what he is seeing. After this moment, the events that follow are sometimes presented out of order, or with gaps between them, and it is up to us as readers to provide our own interpretations from the events described and their **juxtaposition**.

SUPPORTING STORIES

As well as the main plot, involving Amir, Baba, Hassan and Sohrab, there are a number of sub-plots including the stories of the mothers of Amir and Hassan, Rahim Khan and Assef. The most prominent of these is the story of Soraya, Amir's wife. Her story is provided as a complement to Amir's. She, like him, carries a burden of guilt and shame from events in her past. Her role is to show how it is possible to recover from such shame, and so provide hope for Amir.

REVISION FOCUS: TASK 20   A02

How far do you agree with the following statements?

- Telling the whole story in the past tense removes any sense of jeopardy.
- The events of the subplots tell us more about Amir than he does himself.

Try writing opening paragraphs for essays based on these discussion points. Set out your arguments clearly.

CONTEXT   A02

Although not formally split, *The Kite Runner* exists in three sections: Afghanistan, the USA, Afghanistan and Pakistan. A similar three-act structure is often used in film-making: 'set-up', 'confrontation' and 'resolution'.

CHECK THE FILM   A03

The Sixth Sense, starring Bruce Willis (1999), relies on the technique of foreshadowing as a major part of its plot structure.

FORM

GENRE

A FABULOUS STORY

The Kite Runner could be seen as an example of the type of story known as a fable. This is a story, often featuring animals or inanimate objects rather than humans, which is meant to convey a moral lesson. *The Kite Runner* does this by constantly reinforcing what is good and what is bad through Amir's guilt and his need to atone.

STUDY FOCUS: ALLEGORIES   A01

Another way to describe the story would be as an **allegory**. This is a story in which a **metaphor** is expanded out into a whole story so that a smaller **narrative** stands for a larger one. In the case of *The Kite Runner*, Amir's journey of redemption becomes an accompaniment to a description of the trials of the Afghan people; his search for reconciliation can be seen as representative of their search for peace and self-determination.

NARRATIVE TECHNIQUES

AMIR'S STORY

The Kite Runner is written as a single story told to us by the **narrator**, Amir. He is telling it from a point in time at the end of the story, with knowledge of how everything turns out. As a result, all of his recollections are coloured by knowledge of what is to come. This results in a number of narrative techniques being used.

ADULT EYES

One of these can be seen in the fact that a level of adult understanding and rationalising overlays all of the childhood events which we are told about in the first third of the novel. Thus when we are told the stories from Amir's childhood there are two perspectives at work, the child's perception of events, and the reworked and possibly misremembered memories of the adult. As readers we must be aware that the details of the far past may have been changed or granted undue importance in the narrator's mind. This is heightened by the guilt Amir carries over events in his past. As a result it is crucial to notice the number of stories which Amir tells us which paint him in a poor light. He is attempting to portray himself as the 'bad guy' because his guilt tells him he deserves it. This technique is often referred to as 'unreliable narration' whereby we cannot necessarily trust the story we are told by an **unreliable narrator**, or the interpretation that they put on events. As readers we must work to read between the lines and make up our own minds.

CHECK THE BOOK A03

The most famous fables are *Aesop's Fables*, in which moral lessons are told via animals. These fables include: 'The Ant and the Grasshopper', 'The Tortoise and the Hare' and 'The Boy Who Cried Wolf'.

CHECK THE BOOK A03

C. S. Lewis's *The Lion, the Witch and the Wardrobe* (1950) is both a fable – in that it uses animal characters to tell a story with a moral message – and an allegory – with Aslan representing Christ who dies and is resurrected as the saviour of Narnia.

STUDY FOCUS: SHOW AND TELL   A01

The method of storytelling also informs us about the content. Up until the moment of Hassan's rape the stories have largely been related to us as things that happened. They have mostly been 'told' to us, unembellished, in much the way a child relates a story, with the interpretation and emotion of the events explained to us. At the point of fracture that comes with the attack in the alley, the adult voice of Amir takes over and events from then on are largely 'shown' events. By doing this, we are asked to make our own interpretation of how to feel about what unfolds, and so feel more involved in the story.

TALES FROM THE UNCONSCIOUS

Another technique employed to lend depth to the narrative is the inclusion of various dreams. The reporting of dreams is a common technique used in literature. An author may use it to **foreshadow** events to come, with seemingly prophetic dreams; to add a level of **symbolism**; or to provide hidden knowledge that characters are unable to see for themselves. Hosseini uses dreams in the text for all three purposes.

Hassan's dream on the day of the kite-fighting tournament seems to be prophetic of the danger which is waiting for him in the apparently safe day before him; the dream that Amir remembers during the attack on Hassan is symbolic of his feelings of being lost, but also his guilt at being safe; and Amir's later dream, when recovering from Assef's attack, of wrestling the black bear himself, provides the revelation – both to him and to us – that he has finally reconciled himself with his father.

CHECK THE POEM   A03

The use of dreams both as literary device and as a subject is common in literature. In his poem, 'A Dream Within a Dream' (1849), Edgar Allan Poe wonders if life itself is simply a dream.

REVISION FOCUS: TASK 21   A02

How far do you agree with the following statements?

● Amir is too hard on himself for the decisions he took as a child.

● Dreams are used in the novel to tell the reader things about the characters that they don't know themselves.

Try writing opening paragraphs for essays based on these discussion points. Set out your arguments clearly.

LANGUAGE

A CHARACTER'S WORDS

The style of language which an author chooses for a character is created by the structure of their sentences, their choice of vocabulary and the **imagery** they use. These things can reflect the character's level of education, personality type (e.g. enthusiastic, timid), etc. and can also change to show changes in the character.

AMIR'S VOICE

Most of *The Kite Runner* is narrated by Amir. He tells it from the viewpoint of an adult looking back across his life. It is a personal narration in an informal, conversational style, similar to dialogue, rather than a self-consciously literary style of writing.

Amir's **narrative** voice is fairly consistent across most of the novel. However, the vocabulary and sentence structure develop as he moves from talking about his childhood years to talking about his adult life. When relating his childhood, especially in the chapters leading up to the attack on Hassan, he tends to use childlike language, for example, 'he never told on me' (p. 4); or a childlike simplicity of description, 'they clapped for a long time. Afterward, people shook his hand' (p. 13). This style is already starting to show signs of maturity as the narrative reaches the point of Hassan's rape: the trauma of this moment is accompanied by a dropping away of the childlike tone.

Amir's voice also changes at times of stress or anxiety, such as during his fight with Assef and while recovering afterwards. The sentence structure becomes hesitant and broken to reflect the fragmentation of Amir's mind. Following Sohrab's suicide attempt, the narration enters the present tense, resulting in a more urgent and immediate voice: 'They won't let me in. I see them wheel him through a set of double doors and I follow' (p. 300).

CONTEXT A01

A writer's 'voice' is the term describing the individual writing style of a particular author. This can be formed by word choice, grammar, punctuation, but also, at a larger level, by theme, the character's journey and use of dialogue.

STUDY FOCUS: STYLE A01

Turning away from the alley, Amir says 'I was weeping' (p. 67) rather than the more familiar word 'crying'. Then, having decided that he was a coward because he ran away, he tells us that he 'actually *aspired* to cowardice' (p. 68). This is an adult notion and an adult way of expressing it. At the end of that chapter, as he is held and hugged by Baba, he reflects the security he feels in that moment by reverting to a simple childish voice, but this, like the feeling of security that he feels, does not last and by the start of the next chapter the style reverts to a more sophisticated prose with complex **compound sentences**. This style remains for most of the rest of the novel.

OTHER VOICES

CRITICAL VIEWPOINT A02

The phrase 'For you a thousand times over' (p. 59) is one of the key **motifs** of the novel, and a symbol of unquestioning loyalty. When Amir uses this phrase to Sohrab at the end of the novel, we understand the transformation that has taken place in him, from master to servant.

Rahim Khan's voice is a more graceful and less straightforward than Amir's, reflecting his greater age and different temperament. For instance, when talking about Kabul after Amir and Baba left he says, 'No one to greet, no one to sit down with for chai, no one to share stories with, just Roussi soldiers patrolling the streets' (p. 178). This repetitive structure, more like poetry than prose, is typical of Rahim Khan's spoken and written language.

In contrast, Hassan's voice seems to have a more foreign cadence than either Rahim Khan's or Amir's. Of course, Amir's later voice is reflective of a character who has spent many years in the USA, and Rahim Khan's is of an intellectual man who has studied literature. Hassan has learned to read later in life, has only ever lived in Afghanistan and most of his writing and reading, we can assume, would be associated with his religion. Sentences such as 'I am hopeful that one day I will hold one of your letters in my hands and read of your life in America. Perhaps a photograph of you will even grace our eyes' (p. 189) exemplify these aspects.

PART FIVE: CONTEXTS AND CRITICAL DEBATES

HISTORICAL BACKGROUND

THE RULE OF KINGS IN AFGHANISTAN, TO 1973

Throughout the nineteenth century, Afghanistan was largely under the influence of the United Kingdom as part of its occupation of the Indian subcontinent. This was an aspect of what was called the 'Great Game' whereby the Russian and British empires contended for control of the region. This control was maintained by a series of three Anglo-Afghan Wars, which occurred in 1838–42, 1878–80 and in 1919.

Afghanistan finally achieved a measure of independence in 1919 after King Amanullah Khan (whose wife, like Amir's in *The Kite Runner*, was named Soraya) took power and began the move for self-government which started the Third Anglo-Afghan War. Full independence was granted in 1921.

Amanullah Khan's reforms were considered by some as too radical, and he was forced to abdicate in January 1929 by forces led by Habibullah Kalakani, who assumed power. Mohammed Nadir Khan – a cousin of Amanullah – then defeated and killed Habibullah Kalakani just nine months later. This is the man after whom Amir's home district of Kabul was named: Wazir Nadir Khan.

Nadir Khan was assassinated in 1933, and was succeeded by Mohammad Zahir Shah, Nadir Khan's nineteen-year-old son. There followed an extended period of peace in Afghanistan which lasted until former Prime Minister Mohammad Sardar Daoud Khan, the king's cousin and brother-in-law, seized power in a military coup on 17 July 1973.

THE REPUBLIC, UNREST AND CIVIL WAR IN AFGHANISTAN, 1973–92

Afghanistan lasted as a republic under Daoud Khan for just five years. On 27 April 1978 the People's Democratic Party of Afghanistan (PDPA) overthrew Daoud Khan's administration, and he and his family were killed.

In 1979, following a series of uprisings and heavy reprisals, the government of the new Democratic Republic was forced to call on Russian troops to help quell the disturbances. The Soviet Army carried out military missions against US-supported Islamic rebels for the next nine years, finally withdrawing its troops in February 1989. However, the Soviet Union continued to lend aid to the Afghan government until its collapse at the beginning of the 1990s.

CONTEXT A04

The more recent competition in the same area between the USA and the USSR has been called the 'New Great Game'.

CHECK THE BOOK A03

M. E. Hirsh's *Kabul* (1986) is a family's story which starts on the day of the coup and ends with the Soviet invasion in 1979.

THE ISLAMIC STATE OF AFGHANISTAN, 1992–2012

CHECK THE BOOK **A03**

Love and War in Afghanistan (2004) is a set of personal stories about the years of war and oppression from the people of northern Afghanistan, collected by Alexander Klaits and Gulchin Gulmamadova-Klaits.

Without the support of the Soviet Union, the PDPA government was vulnerable and was overthrown on 18 April 1992 by a coalition of resistance fighters. The Democratic Republic was replaced by the Islamic State of Afghanistan. However, following the withdrawal of the common enemy – the Soviet Union – the different groups in Afghanistan turned on each other, creating a civil war between the various classes, ethnic groups, militias, etc.

As a reaction against this fighting, and due to a lack of Pashtun representation in the government, the Taliban, a group of highly religious scholars and fighters, emerged from the southern province of Kandahar. By the end of 2000 the Taliban had control of the majority of the country. The only opposition to them at the time of the attacks on 11 September 2001 was the Afghan Northern Alliance, a small group in the north-east, which continued to be recognised by the United Nations as the legitimate government of Afghanistan.

Following the events of 11 September 2001, the USA and a coalition of allies attacked Afghanistan in an effort to overthrow the government. This was because of the Taliban's refusal to help the USA to find Al Qaeda terrorist forces hiding in Afghanistan and, in particular, to help the search for Osama bin Laden, the man believed to be in charge of Al Qaeda. After the removal of the Taliban government, an interim authority was formed; Hamid Karzai led this authority for six months. At the end of this time Karzai was appointed president by a group led by the former king, Zahir Shah. On 9 October 2004, Afghanistan's first democratic election was held: Karzai was officially voted into the presidency.

At the time of writing, elements of the Taliban and other extremist Islamic groups are still fighting in Afghanistan against the coalition's troops. It would seem that the story of Afghanistan's turmoil is not yet at an end.

LITERARY BACKGROUND

INFLUENCES

The Kite Runner has been described in reviews as representing a new kind of novel, one in which the story of life in Afghanistan has been written by an Afghan but in English, rather than appearing in translation. However, in other ways, *The Kite Runner* is embedded firmly in the history of fiction in the English language. The influence of other texts is reflected in both the plot and the construction of *The Kite Runner* and, whether conscious or unconscious, these **allusions** make the reading of the novel all the richer.

In many ways, *The Kite Runner* is a traditional **realist** novel in which a story is told by a **narrator** with a strong plot which leads the reader through, telling the life of the main character. In this way, the novel is part of a tradition going back to the publication of *Pamela* by Samuel Richardson in 1740, a book often credited as being the first 'real' novel. This book was the story of a maid and her master told through a series of letters, in the form known as **epistolary**. This is a style borrowed by Hosseini for *The Kite Runner* whereby other characters' voices, and some key plot information, are presented to us in letter form.

Charles Dickens's *Great Expectations* (1860–1) would seem to have influenced *The Kite Runner* heavily. As with Hosseini's novel, this is the story of a character's life as narrated by him. However, it is also a story in which an event in the childhood of the narrator has effects for the rest of his life, both internally and externally. In a similar vein is Victor Hugo's *Les Misérables* (1862), which Hosseini actually references in Chapter 24. This too is a novel about a man with events in his past for which he is seeking atonement. It is also a novel in which the historical setting plays a large part.

HISTORY AND WAR

In dealing with the conflicts in Afghanistan, Hosseini aligns himself with other writers who try to make sense of war. These include the famous works of the 'war poets' such as Wilfred Owen or Siegfried Sassoon, and novels such as Sebastian Faulks's *Birdsong* (1993), Michael Frayn's *Spies* (2002) and Pat Barker's *The Ghost Road* (1995). In this respect, and in the setting of much of the novel, *The Kite Runner* can also be seen as an **historical novel**, i.e. one which is set in a period prior to the time of writing. Although the events of the last third of the novel are contemporary to the time of writing, the whole story rests on its historical roots.

POST-COLONIALISM

The most prominent literary antecedents of *The Kite Runner* come in the form of those novels which are considered to be part of the movement known as **post-colonialism**. There are many novels in this category including Arundhati Roy's *The God of Small Things*, which won the Booker Prize for literature in 1997.

In Amir's case – and for Hosseini himself – having been a child at the time of his emigration from Afghanistan, they are in fact similar to the second-generation post-colonial writers who consider their 'homeland' from a greater distance and with a more romantic view. Prominent examples of similar post-colonial fiction include Zadie Smith's *White Teeth* (2000) and Monica Ali's *Brick Lane* (2003).

The Kite Runner's high profile has led to the release of a number of novels dealing with the same subject, and a higher profile in general for books dealing with Afghanistan and other countries which have previously been poorly understood in the West. These include Yasmina Khadra's *Swallows of Kabul* (2002), also set in Afghanistan; Jean Sasson's *Love in a Torn Land* (2007), set amongst the Kurdish people in Saddam Hussein's Iraq; Chimimanda Ngozi Adichie's *Purple Hibiscus* (2004), set in Nigeria; and Rajaa Alsanea's *Girls of Riyadh* (2005), set in Saudi Arabia.

CHECK THE BOOK A03

Ian Watt's *The Rise of the Novel: Studies in Defoe, Richardson and Fielding* (rev. edn 2001) provides an overview of the origins and development of the novel as a literary form.

CHECK THE BOOK A03

A range of different war poetry, including poems by Seamus Heaney, Ted Hughes and W. B. Yeats, can be found in *101 Poems Against War* (2003) edited by Paul Keegan and Matthew Hollis.

CRITICAL DEBATES

CRITICAL HISTORY

FIRST REACTIONS

The Kite Runner (2003), as a still relatively new text, has not yet gained a body of extended literary criticism. It has however been the subject of a number of reviews and profiles and Khaled Hosseini has given interviews about the novel. These form a useful guide to the text and its reception to date.

Initial reviews of a novel try to give the reading public a sense of the storyline of the novel and some indications of whether or not they might like to buy it. This is very different from the intentions of critical writing, which assumes that the reader is familiar with the text and wants to explore it more deeply. However, this does not necessarily mean that reviews are superficial, but simply that they try to deal with the book as a whole, rather than concentrating on individual aspects of it.

The immediate reception of *The Kite Runner*, upon its publication in 2003, was positive, with Edward Hower in the *New York Times* commenting on the 'powerful' nature of the novel, praising it for its ability to mix the personal with the political and the historical: 'Khaled Hosseini gives us a vivid and engaging story that reminds us how long his people have been struggling to triumph over the forces of violence – forces that continue to threaten them even today' (*New York Times*, 3 August 2003).

Many other reviewers also picked up on this aspect of the novel, including Amelia Hill ('An Afghan hounded by his past', *Observer*, 7 September 2003) and Sue Bond ('*The Kite Runner* by Khaled Hosseini', *Asian Review of Books*, 19 July 2003).

However, both Hill and Bond wrote that they thought *The Kite Runner* appeared to be the first novel written by an Afghan in English and aimed at Western readers. This is an opinion which has become accepted as fact. It does, however, ignore *Afghanistan, Where God Only Comes to Weep* by Siba Shakib, published a year earlier. What is certain, however, is that *The Kite Runner* was the first novel of its type to achieve such prominence and to impact so greatly on Western readers.

POPULARITY

According to the author's own website, since its publication the novel has spent over two years on the *New York Times* bestseller list, has been translated into forty-two languages and published in forty-eight countries. Certainly, this widespread readership offers some idea of the popularity of the text. Additionally, in 2006, it was awarded the Penguin/Orange Reading Group (UK) Book of the Year prize.

MORE CRITICAL EYES

The novel has not been free of criticism. David Kipen, reviewing it for Hosseini's local newspaper the *San Francisco Chronicle* on 8 June 2003, pointed out the heavy-handed use of themes in the novel and questioned whether it would have been such a success without the US war in Afghanistan. Both of these seem to be reasonable points which other reviewers appear to have overlooked in their speed to praise a novel hailed as the first of its kind.

CONTEXT A03

The popularity of certain books is increasingly being generated by recommendations from television 'book clubs'. Recommended titles have included Julia Gregson's *East of the Sun* (2008) and Chimamanda Ngozi Adichie's *Half of a Yellow Sun* (2006).

However, a sharper critique of the novel comes in Matthew Thomas Miller's article, 'The Kite Runner critiqued: New Orientalism goes to the big screen'. Miller criticises the novel for promoting the concept of 'new orientalism' (discussed further in the section on **post-colonialism** on page 88) whereby the ruling regimes of the countries of the Middle East are portrayed as cruel and repressive as opposed to the free, liberal and safe nature of the West and, in particular, the USA. While this argument can perhaps be made based upon aspects of *The Kite Runner*, it does neglect Hosseini's attempts to portray the ordinary people of Afghanistan as friendly, intelligent and welcoming, and show the people as the victims of the extremists who are in charge, rather than characterising the whole nation in the same way.

LATER CRITICISM

As time goes on, critics are starting to explore the larger significance of the text. Stephen Chan, for example, in his 2010 article in *Third World Quarterly*, 'The Bitterness of the Islamic Hero in Three Recent Western Works of Fiction', examines the role of the hero in three books, one of which is *The Kite Runner*. His argument is that the reader can only identify with these heroes because they are essentially Western rather then Eastern in their outlook. He says, '[t]hey have become as American as they are Afghan or Pakistani.' (p. 829). This links with ideas of post-colonial literary theory as detailed later in this section.

Taking an innovative approach, Timothy Aubry's article 'Afghanistan Meets the Amazon: Reading *The Kite Runner* in America' (*PMLA*, Vol. 124, No. 1, January 2009, pp. 25–43) examines the reviews of *The Kite Runner* which appeared on the Amazon.com website, to gain an understanding of the popular reaction to the text and how it has impacted on ordinary American readers. He concludes that the empathy American readers feel towards Amir and his emotional journey provides them with a deeper understanding of the humanity of the Afghan peoples, and also some feeling of atonement for their personal guilt over the war in Afghanistan.

CONTEMPORARY APPROACHES

There is no evidence that Hosseini set out to write a novel with any particular basis in the various movements of literary or critical theory. However, he will have been influenced by the books he has read, and by the point in history at which he was writing. A number of different literary theories can therefore be applied to the text in order to achieve greater understanding.

LITERARY MOVEMENTS

The main literary movements in the twentieth century were **modernism** and what can be seen as both its successor and its continuation, **postmodernism**. From the time of its writing, and its setting, *The Kite Runner* falls most clearly in the latter movement, but it is also clearly a part of the movement known as post-colonialism, which encompasses those texts produced either in formerly colonised countries – such as India or Pakistan – or those produced by the emigrants from such countries, such as the Afghans living in the USA, or Bangladeshis living in the UK. In addition, it would be possible to examine *The Kite Runner* from a Marxist perspective, looking at the roles of class and economic power in the novel, or by using the principles of psychoanalysis to examine the way **symbols** and dreams work in the text.

MODERNISM/POSTMODERNISM

The movement known as modernism started in France in the mid nineteenth century, but became more widespread at the beginning of the twentieth century and especially after the First World War. As a literary movement it was a reaction against the **realist narratives** which were the main type of novels in the nineteenth century. These were often epic

CHECK THE BOOK A03

Peter Barry's *Beginning Theory: An Introduction to Literary and Cultural Theory* (2nd edn, 2002) is a useful introductory text for those engaging with critical theory for the first time.

CHECK THE POEM A03

The modernist movement in literature was not solely tied to prose, but was widely explored in poetry as well. The foremost example of this is T. S. Eliot's *The Waste Land* (1922).

CHECK THE BOOK **A03**

A postmodern text that takes the idea of narrative fracture to its logical extreme is Italo Calvino's *If on a Winter's Night a Traveller* (1979), which features ten consecutive opening chapters to ten separate novels.

novels covering long periods of time with an **omniscient narrator** providing their view of events in a linear fashion, for example Jane Austen's *Pride and Prejudice* (1813) and George Eliot's *Middlemarch* (1871–2). Modernism changed this and started to experiment in an attempt to closely examine personal experience, for example Virginia Woolf's 'The Mark on the Wall' (1917) was written as a **stream of consciousness**. Modernist narratives covered much shorter periods of time – for example: James Joyce's *Ulysses* (1922), which is hundreds of pages long, but takes place on a single day – and concentrated on the internal life of the characters via **first-person narrators**.

Postmodernism, as an outgrowth of modernism, maintains many of the features of its predecessor, but also aims to play with these features: fragmented and fractured narratives are used to create meaning from the **juxtaposition** of individual sections of text and the contrast between them. This is evident in *The Kite Runner* when Amir is under stress, such as during the attack in the alley.

The use of an **unreliable narrator** is another postmodern feature of the text. Amir is clearly burdened by his past and we therefore distrust what he tells us and are forced to interpret his words in order to find an 'objective' truth. This makes us question the role of the **narrator** as the source of all information and also highlights the idea that all experience is personal and individual.

POST-COLONIALISM

Although a postmodern novel in certain aspects, *The Kite Runner* can be more easily situated within the tradition of post-colonial fiction as formulated most famously in Edward Said's

1978 book, *Orientalism*. This movement deals with the fiction emerging from countries which were once colonised by others. Said attempted to address the ways in which the West viewed the peoples of Eastern countries as lesser in order to justify their colonisation; such views were reflected in literature and other cultural forms. Post-colonialism examines the way the cultural identity of such a country has been affected by colonisation, and it looks at the attempts to reclaim the cultural heritage made after independence has been gained. It also looks at the texts produced by those people who have left to live in the colonising countries. The ethnic groups formed in these countries are known as the diaspora.

The Kite Runner is a crucial text in this regard because it is one of the first texts written in English by an Afghan dealing with Afghanistan and the many changes of rule and the hardships which its people have suffered. So far there is little critical work on this aspect of the novel, but it would seem to be a rich seam for future exploration.

CHECK THE BOOK **A03**

The perceived return towards 'orientalism', especially post-9/11, is examined in depth in M. Shahid Alam's book *Challenging the New Orientalism: Dissenting Essays on the 'War Against Islam'* (2007).

As a **diasporic novel** written by and about an Afghanistan emigrant, part of *The Kite Runner* examines what it means to be an Afghan in the USA, living as part of an Afghan community which is situated away from the home country. A common feature of this kind of novel is that the community in diaspora becomes a more concentrated form of the society which it has left behind, holding more rigidly to its traditions and customs. *The Kite Runner* describes this phenomenon: the country left behind undergoes such strife and change that the Afghan–American community forms a repository of customs which may be changed or lost in the home country. Amir's return to Afghanistan in the novel allows for a contrast to be drawn between the community in exile and the society remaining in Afghanistan. A useful text to compare *The Kite Runner* with is Anne Tyler's *Digging to America* (2006), which is set in the USA. It describes the mixing of American, Iranian and Korean cultures and also addresses the topic of adoption.

In recent years, especially following the attacks in the USA on 11 September 2001 and the subsequent wars in Afghanistan and Iraq, a 'new orientalism' has been identified by critics who believe that the peoples of those and surrounding countries are being classed once more as 'different' by the Western propaganda surrounding the conflicts. *The Kite Runner*, however, works against this trend by giving the people of Afghanistan a human face. This even extends to the Taliban character of Assef who, while we may not like him or identify with him, we can at least understand as being human and acting from human motives.

MARXISM

Marxist critics examine literary texts in terms of the social and political influences on a work and how these are represented in the finished work. They examine **narratives** to find the distribution of power between different societal groups. In English literature, this often resolves itself as an examination of the wealth and power belonging to the upper classes as opposed to the lack of these things in the working classes. In a novel like *The Kite Runner*, this distinction is drawn on ethnic lines, between the Pashtuns and the Hazaras, as well as the class divides of master and servant.

Examining the way in which religion is used to control the masses is another area of interest for Marxist critics. Amir's people, the Pashtuns, are shown to have less of a respect for religion than the Hazaras: Baba is dismissive, Amir is largely indifferent, and someone like Assef uses his religion as it suits him to further his own ends. Hassan and Sohrab are shown as much more obedient and mindful of their faith and so, according to Marxist theory, exist under a greater degree of control.

PSYCHOANALYSIS

A psychoanalytic approach to literary criticism involves using ideas from Sigmund Freud's and Carl Jung's theories of psychoanalysis. Just as psychoanalysis attempts to identify **symbolism** and concealed meanings in the thoughts and dreams of patients, so the same approach can be taken to literary texts, treating them as the 'dreams' of the writer. Thus, it is possible to read texts in ways which reveal more about both the characters and the writer.

In *The Kite Runner*, a number of aspects become apparent, including the lack of any prominent female figures in the novel. With his mother dead, Amir's journey can be seen in terms of attempting to please his absent mother. He is also seeking a replacement mother figure, which he finds to some extent in the compassionate and understanding side of Rahim Khan.

A repeated symbol is the **motif** of kite flying. This is a child's pursuit, but one still with immense importance for Amir as an adult, suggesting a stunted emotional growth which has never moved beyond childhood.

This kind of analysis could be applied to many aspects of *The Kite Runner*, using a text such as Freud's *The Interpretation of Dreams* (1899). In this book, Freud provides examples of dreams and his method for interpreting them as a way of finding the symbolic nature of dream images and understanding the deeper workings of the mind. The influence of this text can be seen in the way dreams are used in *The Kite Runner* at key moments. Whether it is Hassan's dream of success but also lurking danger on the night before the kite tournament (Chapter 7); Amir's remembered dream of being lost in a snowstorm and then rescued, recounted at the moment of Hassan's attack (Chapter 7); or Amir's dream of himself wrestling his father's black bear (Chapter 23), when recovering in hospital from Assef's beating – all of these dreams are used to symbolise parts of the mind of the dreamer and also the themes of the novel as a whole.

> **CONTEXT** **A03**
>
> Karl Marx was the nineteenth-century German philosopher who co-wrote *The Communist Manifesto*. His main areas of concern were class struggle and the distribution of power and money in society.

> **CONTEXT** **A04**
>
> *The Kite Runner* displays the disparity in wealth and power between Amir and his family, and Hassan and his servants. This reaches its ultimate expression in the 'ethnic cleansing' of the Hazara people during the massacre of Mazir-i-Shairif.

PART SIX: GRADE BOOSTER

ASSESSMENT FOCUS

WHAT ARE YOU BEING ASKED TO FOCUS ON?

The questions or tasks you are set will be based around the four **Assessment Objectives**, **AO1** to **AO4**.

You may get more marks for certain **AOs** than others depending on which unit you are working on. Check with your teacher if you are unsure.

WHAT DO THESE AOs ACTUALLY MEAN?

ASSESSMENT OBJECTIVES	MEANING?
AO1 Articulate creative, informed and relevant responses to literary texts, using appropriate terminology and concepts, and coherent, accurate written expression.	You write about texts in accurate, clear and precise ways so that what you have to say is clear to the marker. You use literary terms (e.g. '**protagonist**') or refer to concepts (e.g. 'a mythical **narrative**') in relevant places.
AO2 Demonstrate detailed critical understanding in analysing the ways in which structure, form and language shape meanings in literary texts.	You show that you understand the specific techniques and methods used by the writer(s) to create the text (e.g. narrative voice, dialogue, **metaphor**). You can explain clearly how these methods affect the meaning.
AO3 Explore connections and comparisons between different literary texts, informed by interpretations of other readers.	You are able to see relevant links between different texts. You are able to comment on how others (such as critics) view the text.
AO4 Demonstrate understanding of the significance and influence of the contexts in which literary texts are written and received.	You can explain how social, historical, political or personal backgrounds to the texts affected the writer and how the texts were read when they were first published and at different times since.

WHAT DOES THIS MEAN FOR YOUR STUDY OR REVISION OF *THE KITE RUNNER*?

Depending on the course you are following, you could be asked to:

- Write about a specific extract and the methods used by Khaled Hosseini in that extract. For example:

How does Hosseini represent how Amir feels about Hassan leaving? (pp. 94–5)

- Respond to a question that challenges you to explore a particular perspective or critical view about the text as a whole. For example:

In what ways can we say that Amir only tells us one version of the story?

- Write about an aspect of *The Kite Runner* that is also a feature of up to two other texts. This may involve comparison between texts, or require that you write about each in turn. For example:

***The Kite Runner* can be seen to be a book about the effects of war. In what ways is its portrayal of war similar to, or different from, *Spies* and *The Ghost Road*?**

TARGETING A HIGH GRADE

Clearly, it is important to know what a high grade answer looks like. It is also important to understand the progression from a lower grade to a high grade. In all cases, it is not enough simply to mention some key points and references – instead, you should explore them in depth, drawing out what is interesting and relevant to the question or issue.

TYPICAL C GRADE FEATURES

	FEATURES	EXAMPLES
A01	You use critical vocabulary accurately, and your arguments make sense, are relevant and focus on the task. You show detailed knowledge of the text.	*Amir is the narrator of "The Kite Runner". This means it is his perspective from which the story is told and he controls the information we are given.*
A02	You can say how some specific aspects of form, structure and language shape meanings.	*Amir is narrating the story from a point in time after the narrative has concluded. This allows him to tie together past and future events to create connections.*
A03	You consider in detail the connections between texts and also how interpretations of texts differ, with some relevant supporting references.	*The question suggests that the novel is about the search for atonement, but as well as seeking to be forgiven for his actions towards Hassan, Amir's journey is surely also about finding a way to live up to his father's legacy. A similar relationship, but reversed can be seen in the father's relationship with the boy in "The Road".*
A04	You can write about a range of contextual factors and make some specific and detailed links between these and the task or text.	*The concept of Western versus Eastern is important in the novel, but Amir is a product of both societies and attempts somehow to reconcile the two.*

TYPICAL FEATURES OF AN A OR A* RESPONSE

	FEATURES	EXAMPLES
A01	You use appropriate critical vocabulary and a technically fluent style. Your arguments are well structured, coherent and always relevant, with a very sharp focus on task.	*Other than two small sections from Rahim Khan and one from Hassan, Amir's is the only voice we hear. As a result the narrative is informed by Amir's sense of guilt with regard to Hassan, and so we must be careful to evaluate the truth of what he tells us.*
A02	You explore and analyse key aspects of form, structure and language and evaluate perceptively how they shape meanings.	*The narrative is structured in a largely chronological order. However, the framing scene which opens the book shows us that Amir is narrating the story from its end point. He is therefore able to link together future and past events from within the story and highlight echoes between these events.*
A03	You show a detailed and perceptive understanding of issues raised through connections between texts and can consider different interpretations with a sharp evaluation of their strengths and weaknesses. You have a range of excellent supportive references.	*Themes of atonement are common in literature, such as Pip's attempts to re-establish his bonds with Joe in "Great Expectations", These themes are very often associated with father-son relationships such as the one between Amir and Baba. Amir's return to Afghanistan is as much about his desire to become the man his father always wanted him to be as it is about reconciling with Hassan's memory. Again, this is similar to Pip's actions towards the end of "Great Expectations". However, Amir's journey is complicated by his desire not only to live up to Baba's wishes but also to become the father to Sohrab that he wished Baba had been to him. In this way he does not simply wish to live up to his father, but also to exceed him.*
A04	You show deep, detailed and relevant understanding of how contextual factors link to the text or task.	*"The Kite Runner" is as much a text about the recent history of Afghanistan as it as about Amir's journey. His story is intimately linked to the fate of his country, with issues such as the split with Hassan and Amir's success in America occurring contemporaneously with major events in Afghanistan. This also works on a metaphorical level with Amir and Soraya's inability to conceive a child acting symbolically for the dubious future for Afghanistan under the Taliban.*

HOW TO WRITE HIGH-QUALITY RESPONSES

The quality of your writing – how you express your ideas – is vital for getting a higher grade, and **AO1** and **AO2** are specifically about how you respond.

FIVE KEY AREAS

The quality of your responses can be broken down into five key areas.

1. THE STRUCTURE OF YOUR ANSWER/ESSAY

- First, get **straight to the point in your opening paragraph**. Use a sharp, direct first sentence that deals with a key aspect and then follow up with evidence or detailed reference.
- **Put forward an argument or point of view** (you won't **always** be able to challenge or take issue with the essay question, but generally, if you can, you are more likely to write in an interesting way).
- **Signpost your ideas** with connectives and references which help the essay flow.
- **Don't repeat points already made**, not even in the conclusion, unless you have something new to add.

TARGETING A HIGH GRADE (AO1)

Let's imagine you have been asked a question about the role of the attack in the alley in *The Kite Runner*. Here's an example of an opening paragraph that gets straight to the point:

Amir's guilt over his refusal to help Hassan during the attack in the alley weighs heavily on him for the rest of his life and acts as a central motif, linking to the wider action of the novel.

> Immediate focus on task and key words, leading to an example from the text

2. USE OF TITLES, NAMES, ETC.

This is a simple, but important, tip to stay on the right side of the examiners.

- Make sure that you spell correctly the titles of the texts, chapters, authors and so on. Present them correctly too, with double quotation marks and capitals as appropriate. For example, *"The Kite Runner"*.
- Use the **full title**, unless there is a good reason not to (e.g. it's very long).
- Use the term 'text' rather than 'book' or 'story'. If you use the word 'story', the examiner may think you mean the plot or action rather than the 'text' as a whole.

3. EFFECTIVE QUOTATIONS

Do not 'bolt on' quotations to the points you make. You will get some marks for including them, but examiners will not find your writing very fluent.

The best quotations are:

- Relevant
- Not too long
- Integrated into your argument/sentence

TARGETING A HIGH GRADE A01

Here is an example of a quotation successfully embedded in a sentence:

When Rahim Khan tells Amir that 'there is a way to be good again' he is finally providing Amir with the chance to atone for his actions as a child.

Remember, quotations can be a well-selected set of three or four single words – such as 'frigid', 'crumbling', 'frozen' and 'deserted' all taken from the first paragraph on page one, painting a bleak and lifeless mood for the opening of the text – or phrases embedded in a sentence to build a picture or explanation, or they can be longer ones that are explored and picked apart.

4. TECHNIQUES AND TERMINOLOGY

By all means mention literary terms, techniques, conventions, critical theories or people (for example, **irony**, **foreshadowing**, **postmodernism** or **post-colonialism**) but make sure that you:

- Understand what they mean
- Are able to link them to what you're saying
- Spell them correctly.

> **EXAMINER'S TIP**
>
> Something examiners often pick up is that students confuse 'narrator' and 'author'. Don't assume that the **'narrator'** in *The Kite Runner* is Khaled Hosseini.

5. GENERAL WRITING SKILLS

Try to write in a way that sounds professional and uses standard English. This does not mean that your writing will lack personality – just that it will be authoritative.

- Avoid colloquial or everyday expressions such as 'got', 'all right', 'OK' and so on.
- Use terms such as 'convey', 'suggest', 'imply', 'infer' to explain the writer's methods.
- Use 'we' when referring to the audience/reader.
- Avoid assertions and generalisations; don't just state a general point of view (*Amir's narration cannot be taken at face value because it is flawed*), but analyse closely with clear evidence and textual detail.

TARGETING A HIGH GRADE A01

Note the professional approach in this example:

Hosseini crafts a text in which events from Amir's childhood are reflected in the events that occur later in his life. The way in which the narrative structure repeats earlier events in new ways brings the reader full circle …

CLOSE READING OF SPECIFIC EXTRACTS

Reading and responding to a specific extract or section of the text is an essential part of your study of *The Kite Runner*. You will be expected to select appropriate information, draw conclusions and make interpretations. When it comes to your exam, you may be asked to focus on a specific part of the text you are studying. For example:

> **How does Hosseini tell the story in Chapter Seven?**

It is important that, from your study, you are familiar with:

- **Where** and **when** the passage/chapter occurs **in the text** (is it the ending of a sequence of events or the actual end of a chapter or key section?)
- What is **significant** about the extract in terms of **the writer's methods (AO2)** (for example, whose voice is it related through? What events or characters are revealed in what order? How is it structured?)

WRITING AN EXAM RESPONSE

You must comment on the **writer's methods** specifically. For example:

DO	DON'T
• Consider **narrative** style and structure, for example, the ways in which the narrative structure fragments when Amir is confronted by the attack on Hassan • Explore Hosseini's use of language, for example: the change from more **lyrical** sentences, such as 'A havoc of scrap and rubble littered the alley' (p. 66), to much simpler, prosaic ones, such as 'Hassan didn't struggle' (p. 66), as the moment of the attack approaches • Think about the importance of setting and how Hosseini portrays it as part of the story (where relevant), for example, his descriptions of the alley • Focus on form, for example: the attack is interspersed with memories of religious ceremonies, which take a different style and form from the rest of the chapter	• Just re-tell the story/plot • Just write about who the characters are and what they do • State what the themes are unless linked to the writer's methods • Micro-analyse – in other words, don't write extensively on just one single word or a particular type of punctuation. This may look impressive, but you need to be sensible about how much impact these particular features may have

There are **two** key things you should do when writing about an extract:
- **Focus** immediately on a specific aspect
- **Develop** your points with detail

For example, in your first paragraph immediately focus on a key aspect of the writer's methods. Don't waste time with general comments or plot summary. Here's an example that gets straight to the point:

> *In the opening to this extract, Hosseini uses the device of a dream to foreshadow events to come.*

In your second paragraph introduce further ideas or develop in more detail your first point. For example:

> *This technique is especially important because it allows us as readers to have some idea what is about to occur, but also shows that Amir, telling the story from after the event, is reaching the heart of his story.*

EXAMINER'S TIP ✓

In further paragraphs you should aim to cover other methods used by the writer and make links between and across the methods. As a whole, your essay should work towards a clear, precise conclusion that directly answers the question.

RESPONDING TO A GENERAL QUESTION ABOUT THE WHOLE TEXT

Alternatively, you may be asked to write about a specific aspect of *The Kite Runner* – but as it relates to the **whole text**. For example:

> **What significance do journeys have in *The Kite Runner* as a whole?**

This means you should:

- **Focus** on **'journeys' specifically** (not other things) and in the plural (i.e. not just one)
- **Explain** their **'significance'** – why they are important, in your opinion
- **Look** at the **whole text**, not just one chapter or extract

STRUCTURING YOUR RESPONSE

You need a clear, logical plan, as for all tasks that you do. It is impossible to write about every section or part of the text, so you will need to:

- Quickly note down five or six key points or aspects to build your essay around:

  Point a *Amir travels from Afghanistan to the USA and back.*

  Point b *When travelling in Afghanistan, Amir suffers from car sickness, yet when travelling in the USA, Amir seems fine, thus indicating that he feels more comfortable in his adopted country than he does in the country of his birth.*

  Point c *The journey back into Afghanistan feels like a journey back into the past, and is important because in order for Amir to achieve resolution in his life he needs to come to terms with his past.*

  Point d *The escape journey from Afghanistan acts like a symbolic birth with the tanker being a womb.*

  Point e *Amir's final journey home with Sohrab is again one of trauma, and significant because once again Amir is faced with tragedy in relation to someone he cares about, but now he has the chance to face it rather than run away.*

- Then decide the most effective or logical order. For example, point **c**, then **b**, **a**, **d**, **e**.

You could begin with your key or main idea, with supporting evidence/references, followed by your further points (perhaps two paragraphs for each). For example:

  Paragraph 1: first key point: *The whole novel is focused around Amir's journey from Afghanistan to the USA and back again.*

  Paragraph 2: expand out, link into other areas: *Each of the trips Amir takes is marked by traumatic events, such as the death of Kamal during Amir's childhood escape in the tanker, and their profound effect on him.*

  Paragraph 3: change direction, introduce new aspect/point: *It is made clear throughout the book that Amir does not travel well. This is significant as it is perceived here as a symbol of his inability to deal with growth and change.* And so on.

- For your **conclusion**, use a compelling way to finish, perhaps repeating some or all of the key words from the question. For example, you could end with:

  Your final point, but with an **additional last clause** which makes it clear what you think is key to the question: *In each of the journeys Amir makes, he learns another lesson which leads him to reconciliation with his past. The final journey home with Sohrab, although marred by the attempted suicide of the boy, marks an end to his wanderings, a chance to be a father, and a chance to finally settle in his chosen home.*

  A **new quotation** or an **aspect** that's **slightly different** from your main point: *However, of all the journeys Amir takes, his most important one is not a physical journey. It is a journey of growth and change which leads to him accept himself and his relationships with those close to him, and to reconcile the mistakes he has made.*

  Or a combination of these endings.

EXAMINER'S TIP ✓

You may be asked to discuss other texts you have studied as well as *The Kite Runner* as part of your response. Once you have completed your response on *The Kite Runner* you could move on to discuss the same issues in your other text(s). Begin with a simple linking phrase or sentence to launch straight into your first point about your next text, such as:
The same issue/idea is explored in much more brutal detail in [name of text] as …

QUESTIONS WITH STATEMENTS, QUOTATIONS OR VIEWPOINTS

Another type of question you may come across is one that includes a statement, quotation or viewpoint from another reader.

These questions ask you to respond to, or argue for/against, a specific point of view or critical interpretation.

For *The Kite Runner* these questions might be worded like this:

- **How do you respond to the idea that 'Assef is no more than an evil villain'?**
- **Some readers argue that *The Kite Runner* is really two novels: one about childhood, the other about adulthood. How do you respond to this view?**
- **How far do you agree with the idea that the character of Amir is presented as unreliable?**
- **To what extent do you think that female characters are important to the novel as whole?**

The key thing to remember is that you are being asked to **respond to a critical interpretation** of the text – in other words, to come up with **your own 'take'** on the idea or viewpoint in the task.

KEY SKILLS REQUIRED

The table below provides help and advice on answering the question:

How far do you agree with the idea that the character of Amir is presented as unreliable?

SKILL	WHAT DOES THIS MEAN?	HOW DO I ACHIEVE THIS?
Consider different interpretations	There will be more than one way of looking at the given question. For example, critics might be divided about the reliability of Amir's narration.	• Show you have considered these different interpretations in your answer. For example: *Amir could be seen as an unreliable narrator or as one that presents us with all the information we require.* *However the answer lies somewhere between the two with Amir providing some information consciously, and some which we can interpret from the way he says it, or from what he leaves out.*
Write with a clear, personal voice	Your own 'take' on the question is made obvious to the examiner. You are not just repeating other people's ideas, but offering what **you** think.	• Although you may mention different perspectives on the task, settle on your own view. • Use language that shows careful, but confident, consideration. For example: *Although it has been said that Amir is an unreliable narrator I feel that he still gives a clear perspective on both his feelings and events from his past, allowing the reader, with careful study, to gain a full understanding of the story.*
Construct a coherent argument	The examiner or marker can follow your train of thought and your own viewpoint is clear to him or her.	• Write in clear paragraphs that deal logically with different aspects of the question. • Support what you say with well-selected and relevant evidence. • Use a range of connectives to help 'signpost' your argument. For example: *However …, And so …, Conversely ….*

ANSWERING A 'VIEWPOINT' QUESTION

Let's turn again to the question above:

How far do you agree with the idea that the character of Amir is presented as unreliable?

STAGE 1: DECODE THE QUESTION

Underline/highlight the **key words**, and make sure you understand what the statement, quotation or viewpoint is saying. In this case:

Key words/phrases = *How far* and *presented as unreliable*

- How far = how much/to what extent/is the evidence mostly/not so much/not at all for this view …
- presented = shown by the writer through thought, speech, action, etc.
- as unreliable = not to be trusted, or capable of error

The viewpoint/idea expressed = *Amir can be seen as an unreliable narrator, but this may not be true throughout the text.*

STAGE 2: DECIDE WHAT YOUR VIEWPOINT IS

Examiners have stated that they tend to reward a strong view which is presented clearly. Think about the question – can you take issue with it? Disagreeing strongly can lead to higher marks, provided you have **genuine evidence** to support your point of view. Don't disagree just for the sake of it.

STAGE 3: DECIDE HOW TO STRUCTURE YOUR ANSWER

Pick out the key points you wish to make, and decide on the order in which you will present them. Keep this basic plan to hand while you write your response.

STAGE 4: WRITE YOUR RESPONSE

You could start by expanding on the statement or viewpoint expressed in the question.

- For example, in **paragraph 1**:

The viewpoint expressed in the question suggests that Amir is an unreliable narrator, meaning that we cannot wholly trust what he tells us and that we must be careful in accepting his version of events. …

This could help by setting up the various ideas you will choose to explore, argue for/against, and so on. But do not just repeat what the question says or just say what you are going to do. Get straight to the point. For example:

… This means that reading the text is not a matter of simple understanding, but also of interpretation as we must assume that Amir's feelings of guilt are colouring his memories of events.

Then proceed to set out the different arguments or perspectives, including your own. You could do this by dealing with specific aspects or elements of the novel one by one. Consider writing one or two paragraphs to explore each aspect in turn. Discuss the strengths and weaknesses in each particular point of view. For example:

- **Paragraph 2** – first aspect:

*To answer whether this interpretation is valid, we need to **first of all** look at …*

*It is clear from this that …/a **strength** of this argument is …*

*However, I believe this suggests that …/a **weakness** in this argument is …*

- **Paragraph 3** – a new focus or aspect:

Turning our attention to … it could be said that …

- **Paragraphs 4, 5, etc. onwards** – develop the argument, building a convincing set of points:

Furthermore, if we look at …

- **Last paragraph** – end with a clear statement of your view, without simply listing all the points you have made:

*To say therefore that Amir is unreliable is only partly true, as **I believe that** while his emotions may affect his narration of his memories, he can still be relied on to be truthful on the details of the main events, which, given their traumatic impact, are likely to be largely consistent.*

> **EXAMINER'S TIP** ✓
>
> You should comment concisely, professionally and thoughtfully and present a range of viewpoints. Try using modal verbs such as 'could', 'might' and 'may' to clarify your own interpretation. For additional help on **Using critical interpretations and perspectives** see pages 100 and 101.

> **EXAMINER'S TIP** ✓
>
> Note how the ideas are clearly signposted through a range of connectives and linking phrases, such as 'However' and 'Turning our attention to …'

COMPARING *THE KITE RUNNER* WITH OTHER TEXTS

As part of your assessment, you may have to compare *The Kite Runner* with or link it to other texts you have studied. These may be other novels, plays, or even poetry. You may also have to link or draw in references from texts written by critics.

Examples of linking or comparison questions are:

- **Explore how writers present emotionally intense relationships in the texts you have studied.**
- **Compare and contrast the importance of journeys in *The Kite Runner* and other text(s) you have studied.**

THE TASK

The question is likely to focus on a method, issue, viewpoint or key aspect that is common to *The Kite Runner* and the other text(s), so you will need to:

Evaluate the issue or statement and have an **open-minded approach**. The best answers suggest meanings and interpretations (plural). Think about the following:

- Do you agree with the statement? Is this aspect more important in one text than in another? Why? How? (How important are journeys to *The Kite Runner*?)
- What are the different ways that this question or aspect can be read or viewed?
- Can you challenge this viewpoint? If so, what evidence is there? How can you present it in a thoughtful, reflective way?

Express **original or creative approaches** fluently:

- This isn't about coming up with entirely new ideas, but you need to show that you are actively engaged with thinking about the question, not just reproducing random facts and information you have learned.
- **Synthesise** your ideas – pull ideas and points together to create something fresh.
- This is a linking/comparison response, so ensure that you guide your reader through your ideas logically, clearly and with professional language.

Know what to compare/contrast: form, structure and **language** will **always** be central to your response, even where you also have to write about characters, contexts or culture.

- Think about standard versus more conventional narration (use of **flashback**, **foreshadowing**, disrupted time or **narrative** voice which leads to dislocation or difficulty in reading).
- Consider different characters' use of language (lengths of sentences, formal/informal style, accent, balance of dialogue and narration; difference between prose treatment of an idea and poem).
- Look at a variety of symbols, images, **motifs** (how they represent concerns of the author/time; what they are and how and where they appear; how they link to critical perspectives; their purposes, effects and impact on the narration).
- Consider aspects of genre (to what extent do Hosseini and the author(s) of the other text(s) conform to/challenge/subvert particular genres or styles of writing?).

EXAMINER'S TIP ✓

Be sure to give due weight to each text – if there are two texts, this would normally mean giving them equal attention (but check the exact requirements of your task). Where required or suggested by the course you are following, you could try moving fluently between the texts in each paragraph, as an alternative to treating texts separately. This approach can be impressive and will ensure that comparison is central to your response.

WRITING YOUR RESPONSE

The depth and extent of your answer will depend on how much you have to write, but the key is to **explore in detail**, and **link between ideas and texts**. Let's use this example:

> Compare and contrast the importance of journeys in *The Kite Runner* and *The Road*.

INTRODUCTION TO YOUR RESPONSE

- Discuss quickly what 'journeys' means, and how well this applies to your texts. This could be meant literally and/or symbolically.
- Mention in support the key journeys that exist in *The Kite Runner* and in *The Road*.
- You could begin with a powerful quotation. For example:

> *'Come. There is a way to be good again' (p. 168) says Rahim Khan in his phone call to Amir. In this simple sentence he is both physically instructing Amir to return to his home country, and also to journey into his past to finally make amends for his childhood actions. In this way, journeying is placed at the heart of the emotional and literal narrative.*

MAIN BODY OF YOUR RESPONSE

- **Point 1:** start with one journey or form of journey in *The Kite Runner*. What does it imply about the war, the community/society as a whole? How does Hosseini uses it to explore the issues of the time? Why was this/wasn't this 'interesting' for readers at the time, and readers now? How might we explore the significance of the journey differently through time and perspective? What do the critics say? Are there contextual/cultural factors to consider?
- **Point 2:** now cover a new factor or aspect through comparison or contrast of this journey with another in *The Road*. How is the journey (or journeys) in this text presented **differently or similarly** by the writer in terms of language, form, structures used? Why was this done in this way? How does it reflect the writer's interests? What do the critics say? Are there contextual/cultural factors to consider?
- **Points 3, 4, 5, etc.:** address a range of new factors and aspects, for example, other types or forms of journey **either** within *The Kite Runner* **or** in both *The Kite Runner* and *The Road*. What different ways do you respond to these (with more empathy, greater criticism, less interest?) and why? For example:

> *While the journey Amir undertakes in the second part of "The Kite Runner" is a return to his beginnings, the journey in "The Road" is about moving away from those beginnings to find something new. In both of these texts the journeys are about seeking ways to lay the past to rest, however this is more possible in "The Kite Runner" than in "The Road". The post-apocalyptic nature of "The Road" means that the past is something to overcome and forget, rather than something to be reconciled with. In this way the past is represented in "The Road" as something to be mourned rather than reclaimed.*

CONCLUSION TO YOUR RESPONSE

- Synthesise elements of what you have said into a final paragraph that fluently, succinctly and inventively leaves the examiner with the sense that you have engaged with this task and the texts. For example:

> *Both of these texts are about literal and metaphorical journeys, but while Amir's journey takes him back to his starting point, and to a chance to become a whole person with his past and future brought together, the journeys of the Man and Boy are ones of loss and bereavement. They therefore display a much bleaker and more pessimistic view than that conveyed in "The Kite Runner".*

EXAMINER'S TIP ✔

Be creative with your conclusion! It's the last thing the examiner will read and your chance to make your mark.

USING CRITICAL INTERPRETATIONS AND PERSPECTIVES

THE 'MEANING' OF A TEXT

There are many viewpoints and perspectives on the 'meaning' of *The Kite Runner*, and examiners will be looking for evidence that you have considered a range of these. Broadly speaking, these different interpretations might relate to the following considerations:

1. CHARACTER

What **sort/type** of person Amir, Hassan, Rahim Khan – or another character – is:

- Is the character an 'archetype' (a specific type of character with common features)? (For example, Rahim Khan can be seen as a mentor/guide character, similar to those found in mythology who assist the heroes with their quests.)
- Does the character personify, symbolise or represent a specific idea or concept, e.g. the mythic hero, the evil foe?
- Is the character modern, universal, of his/her time, historically accurate, etc? (For example, can we see aspects of mythical heroes in Amir? How does he link/connect with characters such as Odysseus or Theseus?)

2. IDEAS AND ISSUES

What the novel tells us about **particular ideas or issues** and how we can interpret these. For example:

- How a society is affected by colonisation
- The role of men/women in different societies
- Moral and social codes, etc.

3. LINKS AND CONTEXTS

To what extent the novel **links with, follows or pre-echoes** other texts and/or ideas. For example:

- Its influence culturally, historically and socially (echoes of the settings, contexts or genres in other texts). (For example, *Great Expectations, Small Island*.)
- How its language links to other texts or modes, such as religious works, myth, legend, etc.

4. NARRATIVE STRUCTURE

How the novel is **constructed** and how Hosseini **makes** his **narrative**:

- Does it follow particular narrative conventions?
- What is the function of specific events, characters, plot devices, locations, etc. in relation to narrative?
- What are the specific moments of tension, conflict, crisis and denouement – and do we agree on what they are?

EXAMINER'S TIP ✓

Bear in mind that views of texts can change over time, even in the space of five or ten years, as values and experiences themselves change, and that criticism can be written for different purposes.

---

5. READER RESPONSE

How the novel **works on the reader**, and whether this changes over time and in different contexts:

● How does Hosseini position the reader? Are we to empathise with, feel distance from, judge and/or evaluate the events and characters?

6. CRITICAL REACTION

How different readers view the novel. For example:

● Different critics over time
● Readers from different countries or backgrounds, e.g. American, English, Afghan

WRITING ABOUT CRITICAL PERSPECTIVES

The important thing to remember is that **you** are a critic too. Your job is to evaluate what a critic or school of criticism has said about the elements listed opposite, arrive at your own conclusions, and also express your own ideas.

In essence, you need to: **consider** the views of others, **synthesise** them, then decide on your **perspective**. For example:

EXPLAIN THE VIEWPOINTS

Critical view A about the concept of Western versus Eastern in the novel:

> *"The Kite Runner" implies that Western ideals of equality are superior to what may be perceived as the more sexist and racist attitudes of Eastern cultures.*

Critical view B about the concept of Western versus Eastern in the novel:

> *In "The Kite Runner" we can see how the after effects of colonisation leave a country unable to achieve stability.*

THEN SYNTHESISE AND ADD YOUR PERSPECTIVE

Synthesise these views whilst adding your own:

> *While the idea that Western ideals of equality are superior could be considered persuasive given the treatment of women and the Hazaras we see in "The Kite Runner", the comment that 'the effects of colonisation leave a country unable to achieve stability' provides an alternative angle allowing for greater understanding.*
>
> *However, I feel that, in fact, "The Kite Runner" may demonstrate a synthesis of these two perspectives, wherein the effects of colonisation, acting alongside existing religious and societal attitudes, work together to produce the oppressive society we see in the text …*

Here are just two examples of different kinds of response to *The Kite Runner*:

● Critic 1 – Meghan O'Rourke argues that the heavy use of **symbolism** and **narrative** techniques in the book detracts from the subtleties of the real situation in Afghanistan, and that this could be a result of Hosseini's ex-patriate status ('The Kite Runner: Do I really have to read it?' *Slate*, July 25, 2005).
● Critic 2 – Edward Hower's review sees the text as a way to examine the larger problems in Afghanistan through the smaller scale of Amir and Hassan's relationship, explaining the political through the personal ('The Servant' *New York Times*, August 3, 2003).

EXAMINER'S TIP

Make sure you have thoroughly explored the different types of criticism written about *The Kite Runner*. Critical interpretation of novels can range from reviews and comments written about the text at the time that it was first published through to critical analysis by a modern critic or reader writing today. With a modern text like *The Kite Runner*, book reviews are especially important as there may not yet be a great wealth of critical commentary built up around the text.

ANNOTATED SAMPLE ANSWERS

Below are **extracts** from two sample answers to the same question at different grades. Bear in mind that these are examples only, using just **AO2** – you will need to check the type of question and the weightings given for the four Assessment Objectives when writing your coursework essay or practising for your exam.

> Question: **How does Khaled Hosseini tell the story in Chapter 7 of** *The Kite Runner*?

CANDIDATE 1

> Do not retell the story; the question asks 'how' it is done

In Chapter 7 of "The Kite Runner", Amir and Hassan are involved in the kite fighting tournament in Kabul. As Hassan runs to find the defeated kite as a trophy for Amir he is attacked in an alley by Assef and his friends. This is all told from Amir's viewpoint, however during the attack – something which Amir witnesses – the narrative becomes fragmented and relates stories not involved in the action. This shows his state of mind.

> **AO2** Good exploration of form and use of language, but needs developing further

> **AO2** A good insight, but use the term **'pathetic fallacy'** to show understanding

> **AO2** Well observed use of contrasting images

The chapter opens with Hassan telling Amir about a dream he had about a monster. It seems to be a good omen, but Amir later sees it as a bad one. Another good omen which Amir seems to see is in the good weather and fresh snow. This is described to show how pure and clean the day is. At first this seems good, but later when Hassan is attacked, it shows a contrast between the beauty of the day and the dirt and horror of the alley. The description of the city is also of a beautiful place. This is very different to how the reader might imagine Kabul from later news photos and descriptions.

> Not strictly relevant

> **AO2** Use the powerful quotation 'We won! We won!' (p. 58) to illustrate

The kite tournament is described excitingly and shows Amir and Hassan in high spirits. This is also in contrast to what comes later. At the moment of triumph, when Amir defeats the other kite, he includes Hassan in the celebration and then sends him off to fetch the defeated kite while Amir is congratulated by the people around him.

> **AO2** Try to avoid repetition of words or phrases ('defeats' and 'defeated')

> Avoid relating too much of the story

> A good observation of character

Amir then searches the streets for Hassan. On his way he asks some people if they have seen Hassan. They are dismissive of Hassan as a Hazara and only seem to help Amir because he is searching for the kite which Hassan has found. This shows the contrast between Amir's opinion of Hassan's ethnicity and that of other people.

> **AO2** A well used quotation to highlight a **motif**

Finally, Amir finds Hassan in an alley, being threatened by Assef and his friends. This description of the alley, and the use of the word 'peeked' echoes the description from the first chapter, informing us that this is the scene that the book has been leading up to. Amir does not enter the alley, but stands and watches the attack.

> **AO2** This is an important point. Say more about Amir's reasons for not rescuing Hassan

Assef doesn't start by physically attacking Hassan, but instead spends time abusing him for being a Hazara and convincing Hassan that Amir is not really his friend, and that he only really sees Hassan as a servant. This could be seen to represent Amir's own thoughts and regrets about his relationship with Hassan, as although Hassan is Amir's best friend, he never tells him so and sometimes bullies him. This means that Amir sees something of himself in Assef and thinks that he is as bad a bully as the other boy.

> This paragraph contains a good observation but it is repetitive and clumsy. Express yourself clearly and concisely

An important observation, but use quotations to illustrate

AO2

A good exploration of language use

During the attack, Amir's attention wanders away from the events he is witnessing and his writing becomes fragmented. This is done to show us that Amir's childish mind cannot cope with what he is seeing. Instead he remembers various events which act as metaphors for the attack on Hassan. He remembers an encounter that he and Hassan had with an old fortune-teller, a dream of being a ghost lost in a snowstorm, and a religious ceremony in which a sheep was slaughtered. When he remembers the sacrificial slaughter of a sheep he says 'I see the sheep's eyes. It is a look that will haunt my dreams for weeks.' However, what he really means is that the look in Hassan's eyes will haunt him, and for much longer than a few weeks.

> **AO2** Ensure you use the correct language. 'Childish' refers to an adult acting like a child; 'childlike' refers to how a child might actually act

> **AO2** What is the significance of the first two fragments?

Good use of a quotation

After the attack, Amir waits for Hassan to come out of the alley. When they meet up, Amir's narration to us tells us how upset he is, and how much he wishes to do something about what he has witnessed, but the way that he talks to Hassan contradicts this.

> **AO2** If talking about use of language, reinforce what you are saying with a quotation from the text

Use a quotation as evidence

At the end of the chapter, Amir finally achieves some sort of reconciliation with his father. This is represented in childlike language. However, we as readers know that this reconciliation can only be temporary as it is based on lies and deceit and this event will become one that Amir regrets later in the book.

> **AO2** Moving off the topic to other chapters. Stay focused

GRADE C

Comment
This answer shows some engagement with the uses of language and structure in the text (AO2) and some attempt to use correct literary terms. However, there is too much retelling of the story, and too many generalities. More use of quotations and specific examples from the text are needed. The answer also needs to explore all aspects of the question, rather than sticking to just a few.

For a B grade
- Focus on examining the story, not retelling it.
- Use illustrative quotations, particularly where talking about language.
- Unpick the ideas that you use, e.g. in what way does the fragmented text reflect Amir's state of mind?

CANDIDATE 2

Clear opening which addresses the question directly

AO2 Good analysis which leads neatly to the next paragraph

AO2 Good use of the correct technical term and the effect it has

Excellent idea and expression of it

In Chapter 7 Hosseini presents us with the central motivation for Amir's story. He introduces the event which has been foreshadowed from the very first chapter – 'I have been peeking into that deserted alley for the past twenty-six years.' – and which gives Amir his reasons for all that he does afterwards. It is written in a variety of styles, from childlike language which reflects Amir's mind at the time of the event, to more lyrical adult language being imposed by him as the narrator.

Amir recalls how the 'streets glistened with fresh snow' with the sky a 'blameless blue', both examples of his adult self narrating and reconstructing the past. It is an example of pathetic fallacy, using the weather to represent an emotion – in this case one of purity and innocence as emphasized by the word 'blameless'. However, this contrasts greatly with the way the alley is described. Amir says: 'A havoc of scrap and rubble littered the alley.' The author's use of the words 'havoc' and 'littered' shows that this is a place not of purity but of chaos, confusion, and discarded items. This might imply that this is place where Amir discards his friendship with Hassan, but perhaps also a disconnection between any sort of spiritual or heavenly influence on the ways of man.

Before the attack itself, Hosseini provides a long description of the kite tournament itself. As it starts, Amir is uncertain whether he will be successful. 'Why was I putting myself through this, when I already knew the outcome?' he wonders. This is an example of Amir's habitual cowardice, however he overcomes it and not only continues to take part but eventually wins the tournament. This is in stark contrast to a similar moment of hesitation when he finds Hassan in the alley. In that case he does not find the bravery to intervene. This juxtaposition of two similar situations shows that gaining the love and respect of Baba is more important to the young Amir than the well-being of his friend.

After the tournament, when Amir is trying to find Hassan, he encounters two Afghans in the streets. They are dismissive of Amir's attempts to find his friend on the basis that Hassan is Hazara. The first, Omar, says he does not know how Hassan can see the kites he chases 'with those tight little eyes.' The second, a fruit seller, seeing that Amir is a Pashtun, asks 'What is a boy like you doing [...] looking for a Hazara?'.

Both of these are graphic examples of the way in which Hazaras were seen as being of less worth than Pashtuns in Afghan society at that time, and from Omar's comment in particular, as being somewhat less than fully human.

AO2 A good use of a quotation, but it is from outside Chapter 7. Remain focused on the topic

AO2 Quotations woven fluently into sentence

AO2 Good examination of language leading to a useful analysis

AO2 Good exploration of contradictions in the text to expose character motivations

AO2

Well argued extrapolation, but extending beyond the chapter in question

It is a motif which is repeated later in the novel when both Farid and General Taheri make similar comments, showing that this opinion of Hazaras has not changed over time.

During the attack, Amir remembers seeing a sheep sacrificed and, by association, this is likened to Hassan. However, the image of Hassan as a sacrifice is prefigured by Assef when, before the attack, he spends some time informing Hassan of how little regard Amir has for his Hazara servant. 'But before you sacrifice yourself for him ...' says Assef, before explaining the various ways in which Amir treats his servant as less than himself. This reflects badly on Amir as we have seen these accusations to be true. However, it contrasts with the previous scene in which Amir is seen as being more progressive than other Afghans. In this juxtaposition we can see that Amir is caught between his nature and the influence of his culture.

AO2

Very good use of language

Expresses a personal opinion on the text clearly

AO2

Good connection to the previous point, whilst moving the argument on

Critical theory not necessary for AO2

In addition to language, the structure of the chapter is also reflective of the events which unfold. At the moment of the attack, Amir's mind moves away from what he is seeing to recalling memories and dreams. This is the second instance of dreams being featured in this chapter, with the first being Hassan's dream of the monster in the lake. By utilising elements of psychoanalytic theory it is possible see how Hosseini, as the author, is able to use this literary device of dreams to present various images to the reader – such as the bond and brotherhood between the two boys expressed in a dream of someone that is presumably Hassan rescuing a ghostly Amir from a snowstorm, or the metaphor mentioned above of Hassan as a sacrificial lamb, being killed so that Amir can continue to lead his sheltered existence, – and also to show that the young Amir is not able to cope with what he witnesses.

AO2

Excellent analysis and linking back to an earlier point

The welcome which Amir receives from Baba when he returns home also implies a stark contrast with the events which have just occurred. Amir's feeling of peace and comfort again shows his desire to shift his mind away from what he has seen. This wish to avoid responsibility will inform his actions for the rest of the book until he is finally forced to confront them by Rahim Khan's phone call.

AO2

Connection to earlier point

GRADE A

Comment
An excellent, clearly written answer which shows great understanding of the uses of language and structure (AO2) in the text and uses clear example quotations to illustrate points. The essay is structured well with a clear argument leading from one concept to another.

To improve this answer
- Stay focused on the question.
- Further, more detailed examination of structure, form and language.
- Consider what is not told, as well as what is. What effect is created by Amir not relating all the details of the attack?

WORKING THROUGH A TASK

Now it's your turn to work through a task on *The Kite Runner*. The key is to:

- Read/decode the task/question
- Plan your points – then expand and link your points
- Draft your answer

TASK TITLE

How do you respond to the idea that 'Assef is no more than an evil villain'? Consider his role in the whole text.

DECODE THE QUESTION: KEY WORDS

How do you respond ...?	= what are **my** views
Assef	= focus on him specifically, not on Amir or Hassan
no more than an evil villain	= he is naturally evil, and his behaviour is totally immoral; he has no other sides or elements to him
whole text	= don't **just** deal with the assault on Hassan

PLAN AND EXPAND

- Key aspect: evidence of Assef being an 'evil villain'

POINT	EXPANDED POINT	EVIDENCE
Point A Assef's treatment of Hassan as a child	● *Assef seems to be a natural bully who is most comfortable tormenting others.* ● *The concept of 'evil' suggests an unchosen, unfaltering state, however Assef can be seen to be a product of his environment.* ● *Assef seems to be worse than his friends, who are uncomfortable with how far he is willing to go.*	'I looked in his crazy eyes and saw that he [...] *really* meant to hurt me' (p. 36) '"It's just a Hazara," Assef said.' (p. 66)
Point B Assef's admiration of Hitler	Different aspects of this point expanded: *You fill in*	Quotations 1–2: *You fill in*
Point C Assef's role in the Taliban	Different aspects of this point expanded: *You fill in*	Quotations 1–2: *You fill in*

- Key aspect: evidence of any other aspects of his behaviour/character

POINT	EXPANDED POINT	EVIDENCE
Point A *You fill in*	Different aspects of this point expanded: *You fill in*	Quotations 1–2: *You fill in*
Point B *You fill in*	Different aspects of this point expanded: *You fill in*	Quotations 1–2: *You fill in*
Point C *You fill in*	Different aspects of this point expanded: *You fill in*	Quotations 1–2: *You fill in*

● Conclusion

POINT	EXPANDED POINT	EVIDENCE
Key final point or overall view *You fill in*	Draw together and perhaps add a final further point to support your view: *You fill in*	Final quotation to support your view: *You fill in*

Now look back over your draft points and:

● Add further links or connections between the points to develop them further or synthesise what has been said, for example:

> *Assef expresses a clear admiration for Hitler. However, this does not, in itself, prove that he is as evil as the man, nor that he is not expressing this opinion in order to unsettle others rather than express a true belief.*

● Decide an order for your points/paragraphs – some may now be linked/connected and therefore not in the order of the table above.

DRAFT

Now draft your essay. If you're really stuck you can use the opening paragraph below to get you started.

> *The character of Assef, although not present for large portions of the novel, stands astride the narrative as a symbol for evil from his first appearance in Chapter 5 where, after being prevented in his bullying by Hassan threatening him with a slingshot, he promises, 'I'm a very patient person. This doesn't end today, believe me'; a promise which lasts throughout the text. He is represented as implacable and unredeemable in his desire to cause harm to Amir and Hassan. However, in addition, he is a reflection of Amir's own dark side and, by providing a physical entity whom Amir can defeat, also allows Amir to defeat the darkness in his own heart.*

Once you've written your essay, turn to page 120 for a mark scheme on this question to see how well you've done!

FURTHER QUESTIONS

1. 'The Kite Runner is a book about fathers and sons.' How far do you agree with this statement?

2. Dreams and memories feature heavily in *The Kite Runner*. Write about their importance in this text and at least one other you have studied.

3. 'Amir and Hassan could never be in friends because of their ethnic backgrounds.' Express your opinion about this statement, focusing on the portrayal of race and ethnicity in *The Kite Runner*.

4. Amir narrates the events of *The Kite Runner* from a point in time after the conclusion of the story. What effect does this have on his narration?

5. 'The Kite Runner is a book which largely ignores religious issues.' In what ways is this statement supported or refuted by the text?

6. The theme of atonement runs throughout *The Kite Runner*. Explore the ways in which different characters are seeking forgiveness for past actions.

7. To what extent is *The Kite Runner* an historical novel?

8. 'Amir narrates his story in a way which favours him.' Discuss the ways in which this statement could be both true and false.

ESSENTIAL STUDY TOOLS

FURTHER READING

BOOKS BY KHALED HOSSEINI

The Kite Runner, 2003

A Thousand Splendid Suns, 2007

FILMS

The Kite Runner, 2007, directed by Marc Forster

CRITICISM

Links to articles and reviews of Khaled Hosseini's work, and an interview with the author, can be found online at **www.khaledhosseini.com**

WAR LITERATURE

Pat Barker, *The Ghost Road*, 1995

Sebastian Faulks, *Birdsong*, 1993

Michael Frayn, *Spies*, 2002

Paul Keegan and Matthew Hollis (eds), *101 Poems Against War, 2003*, including:
Hayden Carruth, 'On Being Asked to Write a Poem Against the War in Vietnam' (from a collection published 1992)

Seamus Heaney, 'Sophoclean', 2003

Ted Hughes, 'Six Young Men', 1957

Philip Larkin, 'MCMXIV', 1964

Wilfred Owen, 'Dulce et Decorum Est', 1917

W. B. Yeats, 'On Being Asked for a War Poem', 1919

POST-COLONIAL FICTION

Monica Ali, *Brick Lane*, 2003

Arundhati Roy, *The God of Small Things*, 1997

Zadie Smith, *White Teeth*, 2000

Anne Tyler, *Digging to America*, 2006

FICTION SET IN AFGHANISTAN

Andrea Busfield, *Born Under a Million Shadows*, 2009

Yasmina Khadra, *The Swallows of Kabul*, 2002

Åsne Seierstad, *The Bookseller of Kabul*, 2004

Siba Shakib, *Afghanistan, Where God Only Comes To Weep*, 2002

OTHER RELEVANT LITERATURE

Jane Austen, *Pride and Prejudice*, 1813

Charles Dickens, *Great Expectations*, 1860–1

Victor Hugo, *Les Misérables*, 1862

BACKGROUND READING

M. H. Abrams, *A Glossary of Literary Terms*, Harcourt Brace, 1981
A useful reference work that covers most common literary terms and provides many articles outlining literary and critical movements

David Ayers, *Modernism: A Short Introduction*, Blackwell, 2004
An introduction to the works of many prominent critics whose theories underpin the study of modernism and postmodernism

Malcolm Bradbury, *The Modern American Novel*, Oxford University Press, 1992, and *The Modern British Novel*, Penguin, 2001
Two books which give an in-depth survey of literary movements and novels written in the English language from the start of the twentieth century

Joseph Campbell, *The Hero with a Thousand Faces* [1949], Fontana, 1993
A book which gives a useful insight into the patterns which stories take, and a way to analyse the various steps of a hero's journey

Paul Cobley, *Narrative*, Routledge, 2003
A clear and comprehensive guidebook to the forms of narrative from the earliest days to its current incarnations in new media

Sigmund Freud, *The Interpretation of Dreams* [1899], Penguin, 1991
A book examining the symbolic meaning of dream images and providing examples of their interpretation

Wendy Knepper, *York Notes Companions: Postcolonial Literature*, York Press and Longman, 2011

David Lodge, *The Art of Fiction*, Penguin, 1992
A book that uses classic and modern fiction to explore the various methods and techniques used by writers

Jessie Matz, *The Modern Novel*, Blackwell, 2004
A useful exploration of both modernism and postmodernism in literature

Michael McKeon (ed.), *Theory of the Novel: A Historical Approach*, Johns Hopkins University Press, 2000
A collection of essays which provides a solid basis for understanding the role of the novel and its place in the history of literature

Edward Said, *Orientalism*, Penguin [1978], 2003
The classic text on post-colonialism

LITERARY TERMS

allegory   a story or a situation with two different meanings, where the straightforward meaning on the surface is used to **symbolise** a deeper meaning underneath. This secondary meaning is often a spiritual or moral one whose values are represented by specific figures, characters or events in the **narrative**

allusion   a passing reference in a work of literature to something outside the text; it may include other works of literature, myth, historical facts or biographical detail

catharsis   the feeling of relief or cleansing that is experienced after going through a traumatic or emotional experience

compound sentence   a sentence which contains one or more sub-clauses as well as the main clause

connotation   the non-literal meanings that become attached to words, such as 'dog' also being able to mean cowardly and lazy, or loyal

contemporary novel   a novel set in the same time period in which the author wrote it

diasporic novel   a text that concerns itself with emigrant societies established in other countries, such as the Bangladeshi community in London featured in novels such as *White Teeth* or *Brick Lane*, or the Afghan community in California seen in *The Kite Runner*

dramatic tension   when a series of events work together to create a need in the reader to find out what happens next

epistolary   the method of telling a story through a series of letters, either from one person to another – giving a single perspective – or between many different participants, giving multiple individual viewpoints

first-person narrator   a **narrator** who is involved in the story being told and can reveal only their own perspective, thoughts and feelings with no access to the thoughts and feelings of other characters

flashback   a scene or event from the past which is related as an aside during a story set in the present

foreshadowing   a literary technique whereby the author mentions events which are yet to be revealed in the **narrative**, either to increase **dramatic tension**, or to provide clues for the reader to attempt to guess what will happen next

historical novel   a novel set in a time period prior to the time in which the author wrote it, in which the cultural/social/political events of that period play a significant part in the story

imagery   descriptive language which uses images to make actions, objects and characters more vivid in the reader's mind. **Metaphors** and similes are examples of imagistic language

irony   the humorous or sarcastic use of words to imply the opposite of what they normally mean; incongruity between what might be expected and what actually happens; the ill-timed arrival of an event that had been hoped for

juxtaposition   the technique of placing two or more seemingly unrelated ideas next to each other in a text, creating meaning from the interaction of the differences and similarities between them

lyrical expressing thoughts and feelings in an imaginative and beautiful way; often used to describe poetry, or prose that can be seen as beautiful or poetic

metaphor a figure of speech in which a word or phrase is applied to an object, a character or an action which does not literally belong to it, in order to imply a resemblance and create an unusual or striking image in the reader's mind

modernism a literary movement which moves away from traditional **realist** forms of writing to embrace experimental forms and a more personal perspective

motif a recurring idea in a work, which is used to draw the reader's attention to a particular theme or topic

narrative a story, tale or any recital of events, and the manner in which it is told. First-person narratives ('I') are told from the character's perspective and usually require the reader to judge carefully what is being said; second-person narratives ('you') suggest the reader is part of the story; in third-person narratives ('he, 'she', 'they') the narrator may be intrusive (continually commenting on the story), impersonal, or omniscient. More than one style of narrative may be used in a text

narrator the voice telling the story or relating a sequence of events

omniscient narrator a **narrator** who uses the third-person narrative and has a god-like knowledge of events and of the thoughts and feelings of the characters

pathetic fallacy the attribution of human feelings to objects in nature and, commonly, weather systems, so that the mood of the **narrator** or the characters can be discerned from the behaviour of the surrounding environment

post-colonialism a branch of literary theory which examines the texts written by authors from formerly colonised countries with regard to how the culture of such countries have been changed by colonisation and examining the process of recovery and regaining of cultural identity

postmodernism a literary movement which, in reaction to modernism, introduces more experimental ways of writing. Postmodern writing often plays with established forms as a way of commenting on them, or uses many different forms in a single work, mixing high and low culture, in an attempt to create a literature without boundaries

protagonist the principal character in a work of literature

realism a literary movement of the second half of the nineteenth century which attempted to depict everyday life in unromanticised terms, sometimes describing everyday activities in detail and attempting to tell stories of 'real' lives

stream of consciousness writing which presents thoughts as they occur to a character or narrator in a constant flow with no overt attempts to link or structure them

symbolism investing material objects with abstract powers and meanings greater than their own; allowing a complex idea to be represented by a single object

synecdoche a language effect where a part of an object represents the whole, for example, the Crown represents the Queen and the whole royal family

unreliable narrator a first-person **narrator** who does not necessarily always give the reader complete or accurate information, or whose personal feelings influence their interpretation of the events as narrated

TIMELINE

WORLD EVENTS	LITERARY EVENTS	KHALED HOSSEINI'S LIFE
	1740 Publication of *Pamela* by Samuel Richardson	
	1813 *Pride and Prejudice* by Jane Austen	
	1860–1 *Great Expectations* by Charles Dickens	
	1871–2 *Middlemarch* by George Eliot	
1914–18 First World War	**1917** 'Anthem for Doomed Youth' by Wilfred Owen	
1919 Treaty of Versailles establishes the grounds of peace after the First World War and Afghanistan is granted a measure of independence		
1921 Afghanistan achieves full independence under King Amanullah Khan		
	1922 *Ulysses* by James Joyce	
	1924 *A Passage to India* by E. M. Forster	
	1927 *To the Lighthouse* by Virginia Woolf	
1929 King Amanullah Khan is forced to abdicate by Habibullah Kalakani, who assumes power. He, in turn, is deposed nine months later by Mohammed Nadir Khan		
1933 Mohammed Nadir Khan is assassinated and is succeeded by his son Mohammad Zahir Shah		
1939 Outbreak of Second World War		
1945 End of Second World War; dropping of atomic bombs on Nagasaki and Hiroshima in Japan		
1945–91 Cold War		
	1955 *Lolita* by Vladimir Nabokov	
		1965 (4 March) Born in Kabul, Afghanistan
	1969 *The French Lieutenant's Woman* by John Fowles	
		1970 Family moves to Tehran, Iran
1973 Prime Minister Mohammad Sardar Daoud Khan, the king of Afghanistan's cousin and brother-in-law, seizes power in a military coup		**1973** Family moves back to Kabul
		1976 Family moves to Paris
1978 The People's Democratic Party of Afghanistan (PDPA) overthrows Daoud Khan's government	**1978** *Orientalism* by Edward Said	

WORLD EVENTS	LITERARY EVENTS	KHALED HOSSEINI'S LIFE
1979–89 Russian troops occupy Afghanistan lending aid to the government against the Mujahedin	**1981** *Midnight's Children* by Salman Rushdie	**1980** Family seeks political asylum in the USA and settles in San Jose, California
		1984 Graduates from Independence High School in San Jose, California
		1988 Gains a degree in biology from Santa Clara University, California
	1989 *London Fields* by Martin Amis	**1989** Joins the University of California, San Diego, School of Medicine
1990–1 The Gulf War between UN coalition and Iraq following Iraq's invasion of Kuwait		
1992–2001 Under the new Islamic State of Afghanistan, the Taliban slowly take control of Afghanistan		
	1993 *Birdsong* by Sebastian Faulks	**1993** Becomes a medical doctor and joins a residency programme in internal medicine at Cedars-Sinai Medical Center in Los Angeles
		1996 Completes his residency and becomes a practising doctor
	1997 *The God of Small Things* by Arundhati Roy	
	2000 *White Teeth* by Zadie Smith	
2001 onwards Following the attacks on the USA on 11 September 2001, a coalition of countries invades Afghanistan in an effort to find Al Qaeda operatives. They overthrow the rule of the Taliban who become a guerilla force attempting to oust the invaders		**2001** Starts writing *The Kite Runner*
	2002 *Afghanistan, Where God Only Comes to Weep* by Siba Shakib	
2003 USA and UK invade Iraq for the second time	**2003** *Brick Lane* by Monica Ali	**2003** *The Kite Runner* is published
2004 Hamid Karzai is voted president of Afghanistan		
		2006 Named a Goodwill Envoy for NHCR
		2007 Release of *The Kite Runner* (film); *A Thousand Splendid Suns* is published
	2008 *The Inheritance of Loss* by Kiran Desai	

REVISION FOCUS TASK ANSWERS

TASK 1

Amir is the most important character in the novel.

- Amir is the narrator – the story is all from his viewpoint.
- He is also the protagonist – it is his journey we are following.
- However, the novel is named after Hassan who is, arguably, the reason for everything Amir does.

The Kite Runner is told from Amir's point of view, based on his memories and emotions, and we cannot entirely trust what he tell us.

- Amir provides us with all of the information, yet his feelings of guilt colour his memories.
- The truth of what Amir as narrator tells us can be judged against other accounts – e.g. the small sections from Rahim Khan and Hassan.
- As readers we need to interpret what we are being told to see if there are alternative explanations to those offered.

TASK 2

The way Amir describes his friend makes us like Hassan more than we like Amir.

- In writing a first person narrative, Amir focuses more on others than on himself.
- Hassan is at the centre of the novel, therefore it is important that he is painted positively.
- We can see this as an example of Amir's feelings of guilt, and the resulting dislike of himself, colouring his memories.

The Kite Runner is a novel that examines the way the events of history cannot be escaped.

- Historical events are entwined throughout the novel with the personal ones.
- Amir is focused on the misdeeds of his childhood, therefore his focus is on the past rather than the present.
- As *The Kite Runner* is a novel about Afghanistan, it is important that readers understand the context and the impact this has on events.

TASK 3

The use of stories within *The Kite Runner* reminds us that we are reading a work of fiction rather than a true account.

- While the events of the novel may not have happened, this does not mean that they cannot help us to greater understanding of the issues they raise.
- Literature sometimes claims to show us the truth about human nature through a fictional account.
- All stories, non-fiction or fiction, are told by a person who has a subjective viewpoint.

Understanding the role of religion is key to understanding the whole text.

- Hassan and Amir are shown to be greatly different in how they relate to their religions.
- The history of much of the strife in the middle-East is based around the Shi'a/Sunni divide.

TASK 4

The Kite Runner is an historical novel.

- Definite historical events are referenced in the text.

- The story seems to work, at least in part, to educate the reader about Afghanistan.

- While much of the text takes place in the recent past, the events narrated – such as the attacks on 11 September 2001 – will undoubtedly be featured in future history books.

Amir is a worse bully than Assef.

- Amir is scared. This makes him dislike himself, and then take this anger with himself out on Hassan.

- Amir feels guilt about what he does. Assef is not shown to feel any guilt.

- Amir should be Hassan's friend, therefore his bullying can be seen as being more hurtful.

TASK 5

The style of writing changes throughout the novel depending on the emotions being felt by Amir.

- In the opening sections the style is childlike and mostly optimistic, reflecting a time before the attack.

- At the point of the attack there are childlike elements mixing with more adult phrases, suggesting a point of transformation.

- During the fight with Assef at the end of the novel, Amir's voice regains some of the earlier optimism.

The events in the alley make Amir the person he becomes.

- In part the events in the alley actually seem to ruin Amir's life and stunt his development.

- The guilt that Amir feels over not acting to help Hassan make him a compassionate and driven man.

- We are all the products of our experiences, and it can be argued that the more traumatic ones have a greater effect.

TASK 6

The message of *The Kite Runner* is that it is better to tell the truth than keep secrets.

- Amir's secrets are a source of great psychological harm to him; likewise, Baba is scarred by the secrets he keeps.

- Keeping secrets can protect other people and allow them to make their own decisions – such as Rahim Khan not revealing Amir's and Baba's secrets earlier.

- There could be other messages such as the power of forgiveness and redemption.

The novel demonstrates that our natures are formed by the people around us.

- Much of Amir's personality is a reaction to his father both in terms of emulation and rebellion.

- However, Amir gained a great part of his nature from his absent mother.

- Hassan is very similar to Ali in nature, despite being Baba's son.

TASK 7

The novel demonstrates that stories reflect the world back to us.

- Amir writes his stories as a way of understanding both the world and himself.
- The whole text itself is a creation by Amir.
- The storybook which Amir reads to Hassan and to Sohrab contains stories with moral messages from which they learn.

A compelling story must include examples of both good and evil.

- Amir undertakes actions which could fall into both categories.
- Without Assef as a representation of true evil, the novel would lack power.
- Examples of good and evil embodied in individuals can act as metaphors for good and evil within society.

TASK 8

The novel suggests that the past should never be forgotten.

- Amir attempts to put his past behind him, but without reconciliation he cannot.
- The events of the past – both personal and global – make up a large part of how characters react to future events.
- Remembering and dealing with the past allows the characters to move forward in life.

Love is the most important emotion in *The Kite Runner*.

- Amir's journey is a search for love – from Baba, Hassan, Soraya and Sohrab.
- Amir is also driven by fear, guilt and a search for forgiveness.
- It is a mixture of emotions that makes the characters fully human.

TASK 9

The novel suggests that our ability to learn is what separates mankind from animals.

- Amir's refusal to teach Hassan to read suggests Amir sees the other boy as less human than he is.
- Amir's education allows him to become a respected member of society.
- At the end of the story Amir is finally able to learn from his actions and not keep repeating the same things over again.

Amir's experiences demonstrate that home is where you choose to make it.

- For Amir, Afghanistan can be seen as his first and truest home.
- Amir seems more comfortable and settled in the USA than he did in Afghanistan.
- Once Amir becomes comfortable with himself, he becomes comfortable in the world.

TASK 10

Rahim Khan's call gives meaning to Amir's life.

- Amir has been living as if he were waiting for the call.
- Once Amir has responded to the call and decided on action, it is as though his life has finally begun.
- Rahim Khan gives Amir the chance to redeem his mistakes and, to some extent, rewrite his past.

The Kite Runner demonstrates that forgiveness is important.

- His search for forgiveness is what drives Amir.
- Learning that Baba was also Hassan's father allows Amir to forgive his father.
- Having saved Sohrab and finally faced his fears, Amir is able to forgive himself.

TASK 11

The Kite Runner is actually a novel about children.

- The important events occur to Amir and Hassan when they were children.
- Amir and Soraya's childless state is reflective of Amir's failure to grow up.
- The saving of Sohrab is the key to Amir finally achieving closure.

The absence of female characters in the novel is as important as the presence of so many male ones.

- The lack of a mother for Amir makes the tension between him and Baba worse than it might have been.
- Likewise, the absence of Sofia makes it harder for Baba to relate to Amir.
- Sanaubar's absence also has an effect on Hassan. Her return prompts a reconciliation in his own life.

TASK 12

The novel suggests that secrets should always be revealed.

- If Baba had been open about being Hassan's father, Amir would not have felt as he did towards his father.
- If Rahim Khan and/or Amir had spoken of Hassan's attack, Amir would not have had a life filled with guilt.
- The characters in the novel keep secrets because the truth is too painful or shameful to reveal.

The Kite Runner is a novel about cities.

- Cities are places of progress and the centres of power.
- The events of the novel take place, almost entirely, in the cities of Kabul, San Jose, San Francisco, Peshawar and Islamabad.
- Comparisons are formed between the various cities, and between the East and the West.

TASK 13

The state of Afghanistan on Amir's return is symbolic of his feelings over the deaths of Baba and Hassan.

- For Amir, the loss of his father and brother means that Afghanistan has lost a lot of its magic, whatever state it is in.
- With his protectors now both dead, Amir has to deal directly with the world, even the ugly parts.
- Death of a loved one often causes memories to come to the surface. In this way a return to Afghanistan is a journey into memory for Amir.

Amir's car sickness is psychological, i.e. all in his head.

- Amir is only car sick in Afghanistan. There is no record of it in the USA.
- The car sickness only seems to occur when Amir is stressed or anxious.
- In the final journey through Afghanistan after saving Sohrab, Amir reports no car sickness.

TASK 14

Even though he is an adult when he returns to Afghanistan, Amir is still essentially a child.

- Amir is fixated on the events from his childhood and still sees them as influencing him.
- Instead of dealing directly with Wahid, Amir resorts to hiding money under the mattress, just as he did as a child.
- Amir shows his naivety in his reaction to seeing the Taliban on the streets of Kabul.

The events in this section of the novel suggest that the people of Afghanistan have become used to the rule of the Taliban.

- The reaction on the streets of Kabul when the Taliban pass is one of familiarity despite the threat.
- Amir, an outsider, is the only member of the crowd at the football stadium appalled by what happens.
- However, Farid's reaction to Amir saving Sohrab is one of great admiration, suggesting that Afghans are doing what they need to do to survive, but are not resigned to the rule of the Taliban.

TASK 15

The novel suggests that great change requires great suffering.

- Amir suffers at the hands of Assef, but defeats his demons in the process.
- Assef himself also mentions being badly beaten and taking it as a message from God which set him on his path.
- It remains to be seen whether Afghanistan's sufferings will lead to a better country.

Assef has been as successful, in his own way, as Amir.

- Assef has risen high in the Taliban.
- Goals which Assef had as a child to be a leader have come to fruition.
- Within a much more difficult society than Amir's home in the USA, Assef has achieved a life of luxury.

TASK 16

Amir is an unconventional Afghan.

- Even as a child, Amir does not see the same distinction between Pashtun and Hazara as most other Afghans.
- He finds he is more at home in the USA than in Afghanistan.
- He does not seem to have the same obstinate pride as many Afghans.

The Kite Runner is a novel with a 'happy' ending.

- Amir finally receives closure for the events which have plagued his life.
- Despite his great losses and traumas, there seems to be hope for happiness in Sohrab's life.
- However, Amir's one small victory makes no great difference to Afghanistan's plight.

TASK 17

Amir's search for redemption is also a search for the lost love of his mother.

- The lack of a mother in Amir's life can be seen as the source of his inability to deal with emotions.
- Amir's reaction to Rahim Khan is to the man's more caring side. His willingness to return and carry out the man's wishes can be seen as seeking reconciliation with a lost mother.
- Unable to find a mother's love and unable to become a natural parent, the chance to be a father to Sohrab is the way to replace that lost love.

Amir could not truly become a man while Baba was still alive.

- Much of Amir's childlike nature is a reaction against the stature of his father.
- Even after his marriage, Amir still lives with his father, only becoming head of the household once Baba dies.
- Baba protects Amir from life. Only once this protection is removed does Amir have to face things for himself.

TASK 18

Hassan is more Ali's son than Baba's.

- Hassan is recognisably a Hazara.
- Hassan has a similar demeanour to Ali from having been brought up and taught by him.
- However, Hassan has a similar physicality to Baba.

TASK 19

When Rahim Khan calls Amir back to Pakistan he is seeking atonement for his own silence over Hassan's attack.

- Despite the passage of time, when Rahim Khan learns he is dying, he sees it as time to help Amir to atone for his past.
- Rahim Khan must have known that his failure to speak up caused pain to Amir, Hassan and Baba.
- Tricking Amir into having to adopt Sohrab is Rahim Khan's attempt to put things back as they were.

TASK 20

Telling the whole story in the past tense removes any sense of jeopardy.

- Because the story is told from its end point, we know that Amir will survive whatever happens to him.
- However, we do not know what trials and traumas Amir may suffer, so jeopardy is maintained.
- Also, we do not know what might befall other characters.

The events of the subplots tell us more about Amir than he does himself.

- In talking about Baba and his exploits, Amir reveals feelings for his father of love, awe, jealousy and fear.
- In talking about Soraya's past, Amir reveals how much his own past weighs on him.
- However, Amir is intelligent and self-aware, so does analyse his own feelings and motivations as well.

TASK 21

Amir is too hard on himself for the decisions he took as a child.

- The story is told by an adult Amir criticising his younger self for decisions taken because of fear.
- Due to Hassan and Ali leaving, followed by Baba and Amir fleeing Afghanistan, Amir did not have a chance to put things right.
- However, if we can trust what Amir says, then readers will probably feel that Amir should have spoken up when he had the chance.

Dreams are used in the novel to tell the reader things about characters that they don't know themselves.

- Hassan's dream about the monster in the lake shows his optimism and his love for Amir.
- Amir interprets the same dream differently later, seeing himself as the monster.
- When Amir dreams about himself becoming the person fighting the bear we can see him coming to terms with achieving a similar stature to Baba.

MARK SCHEME

Use this page to assess your answer to the **Worked task**, provided on pages 106–7.

Aiming for an A grade? Fulfil all the criteria below and your answer should hit the mark.*

> **How do you respond to the idea that 'Assef is no more than an evil villain'? Consider his role in the whole text.**

AO1	Articulate creative, informed and relevant responses to literary texts, using appropriate terminology and concepts, and coherent, accurate written expression.	● You make a range of clear, relevant points about Assef's character as evil and villainous. ● You write a balanced essay covering both positions. ● You use a range of literary terms correctly, e.g. **foreshadowing**, **catharsis**, theme, **imagery**, **irony**, **symbolism**. ● You write a clear introduction, outlining your thesis and provide a clear conclusion. ● You signpost and link your ideas about Assef's character as evil and villainous.
AO2	Demonstrate detailed critical understanding in analysing the ways in which structure, form and language shape meanings in literary texts.	● You explain the techniques and methods Hosseini uses to present Assef's character as evil and villainous and link them to main themes of the text. ● You may discuss, for example, the ways in which Assef talks at Amir's birthday party. His comments are not very far removed from things said by many of the Afghan population, including characters such as Farid whom Amir meets upon his return. However, Assef's references to Hitler make his comments more ominous. ● You explain in detail how your examples affect meaning, e.g. the presentation of the Hitler biography as a gift – with books having a special significance to Amir with his love of stories and writing. ● You may explore how the setting – the alley – contributes to the presentation of evil.
AO3	Explore connections and comparisons between different literary texts, informed by interpretations of other readers.	● You make relevant links between Assef and the concept of evil, noting how the description of the former interacts with commentary on the latter. ● You could discuss the idea of the stock villain in other texts, e.g. Shakespeare's plays, the role of this character 'type' and how this corresponds to Assef. ● When appropriate, you compare Assef's presentation with the presentation of evil villains in other text(s), e.g. Heathcliff's treatment of Isabella and Linton in *Wuthering Heights*. ● You incorporate and comment on critics' views of how evil and villainy are presented in the novel. ● You assert your own independent view clearly.
AO4	Demonstrate understanding of the significance and influence of the contexts in which literary texts are written and received.	You explain how relevant aspects of social, literary and historical contexts of *The Kite Runner* are significant when interpreting expressions of Assef's character as evil and villainous. For example, you may discuss: ● Literary context: in any text of a redemptive quest, there must be a 'monster' for the hero to overcome. Assef can be seen as this monster. ● Historical context: Assef, as a member of the Taliban, stands in for their whole regime. In this way, Amir's battle against him is a battle against Afghanistan's problems. ● Social context: Assef can be seen as the natural product of a sick society in which some people are seen as being 'better' than others, such as the traditional treatment of the Hazaras by the Pashtuns.

* This mark scheme gives you a broad indication of attainment, but check the specific mark scheme for your paper/task to ensure you know what to focus on.